A House in the Shadows

Maria Messina

A House in the Shadows

Afterword by Annie Messina

Translated by John Shepley

The Marlboro Press

First English language edition.

Translation copyright © 1989 by John Shepley.

Originally published in Italian as
LA CASA NEL VICOLO
Copyright © 1982 by Sellerio Editore, Palermo.

The publication of the present volume is made possible by a grant from the National Endowment for the Arts.

Manufactured in the United States of America.

Library of Congress Catalog Card Number 89-60939

Cloth: ISBN 0-910395-50-0
Paper: ISBN 0-910395-51-9

THE MARLBORO PRESS

MARLBORO, VERMONT

This translation is dedicated to
Claude Choquet
who discovered Maria Messina in Tours.
—J.S.

Contents

A House in the Shadows

I

NICOLINA was sewing on the balcony, hastening to make the last stitches in the dim twilight. The view offered by the high balcony was enclosed, almost smothered, between the narrow little street, which at that hour looked as dark and deep as an empty well, and the broad expanse of reddish, moss-covered roofs over which a wan sky hung low. Nicolina sewed quickly, without lifting her eyes: she felt the monotony of the constricted landscape as though it were part of the air she breathed. Unwittingly her thoughts kept going back to the house in Sant'Agata; she saw again the little balcony of rusted iron that overlooked the fields, under the open sky whose clouds seemed to merge with the sea, far away.

For Nicolina, this was the most restful, if most melancholy, hour of the day. All her chores were done. In the house, as in the air, and within her soul, there was a pause, a mournful silence. Then it seemed that her thoughts, regrets, and hopes came forward bathed in the same uncertain light that illuminated the sky. And there was no one to interrupt her vague, unfinished soliloquies.

Antonietta was in the bedroom, at the bedside of Alessio, who for six days had been running a fever. Her brother-in-law, as usual, had remained seated at the table, which Nicolina had cleared. In the semidarkness of the room, you could see the coal in his long pipe glowing like a little red dot. After eating supper—and they ate while it was still light so as not to go to bed on a full stomach—he smoked for exactly one hour (the clock's pendulum swung back and forth at the center of the wall), keeping his eyes placidly half-closed.

Night was falling, and the last light had faded. Nicolina put her work back in the basket, and rather reluctantly stood up. She had to prepare the glass of water that her brother-in-law was wont to sip slowly, two hours after his supper. Antonietta, in her concern for the sick boy, would have neglected to do so.

She squeezed slightly less than half a lemon into the water, taking care that no seeds fell with the juice; she added just enough wine to tinge the water, dissolved in it a level teaspoonful of sugar, shook it, stirred it, and let it settle. Then she held the glass up to the light to make sure the drink was perfectly limpid, the way Antonietta prepared it. And finally, cautiously, she brought the glass on a saucer.

She went back to the balcony. But her brother-in-law immediately called her.

"You want to get sick too? It's damp outside."

Nicolina would have liked to explain that the air seemed unusually warm to her. But she came back inside without replying.

"Close it."

Sighing, she closed the French door halfway.

"Close it properly."

She closed the shutters as well, noiselessly. She remembered how her father, who didn't like to shut the blinds completely, used to say: "When a tired traveler gets to a village at night, it makes him feel better to see a little light in the houses . . ."

She sat down at the table and resumed her sewing, trying not to disturb her brother-in-law by the movement of her hand drawing the needle. Carmelina, having brought her toys close to her aunt, began to rock a doll made from a few rags and a piece of string, singing softly, "Let's go bye-bye . . ." But she quickly stopped and fell silent, looking a little fearfully at her father.

Then Antonietta came in, pale and worried, and she too sat down.

"I'm so glad you thought of the lemonade," she whispered in her sister's ear.

"You weren't coming . . ."

"I was sure you'd take care of it." Still in a whisper, caressing the little girl, she added, "Don't you think it's time you went to bed? I have to go back in there."

"Just as soon as I finish this seam."

They were silent. When Don Lucio was at home, they usually kept quiet while they worked, so as not to disturb him.

Antonietta, whose whole being exhibited a painful anxiety, twice broke the heavy silence with a deep sigh. Each time Nicolina raised her eyes from her work and looked at her with concern.

Don Lucio was savoring his pipe with an almost voluptuous satisfaction. His eyes half-closed, he followed

3

every little movement made by the two sisters. In their expressions, their ways of moving and looking, they both showed the same embarrassment, the same clumsiness, born of their constant and mysterious fear of being a nuisance to him. He felt a renewed pleasure every time he noticed how profound an influence he had on the two women, especially on Nicolina, who in the beginning had shown an almost exuberant and unpleasing vivacity.

Nicolina rose, and Carmelina followed her after hurriedly kissing the stiff, cold hand that her father, without pausing in his smoking, held out to her every evening.

"Bring my papers and spectacles."

Antonietta brought to the table the briefcase bulging with ledgers, and the box with the pens and inkwell, which were neatly arranged on a small shelf near the window. Don Lucio watched with satisfaction as his wife made two trips back and forth. Admiring the supple movements of his woman's strong full hips, he was pleased with himself, just as he was pleased every time he paused to contemplate the expensive furniture with which he had embellished his house.

Nicolina came back. "I looked in on Alessio," she said. "He's moaning in his sleep."

Antonietta gazed imploringly at her husband. She went out, then returned immediately on tiptoe. "Lucio!" she called timidly, standing in the doorway, a sob in her voice. "I think he's worse!"

He pretended to get angry. "Do you enjoy bothering me, you two?" he shouted. "Spoiling my few minutes of rest after a hard day's work?"

Antonietta went back to the bedroom, humiliated

4

and distressed. He never believed her when she told him her fears!

"It's my own fault," she confessed to her sister. "I'm always so tactless in saying things . . ."

"Would you like me to talk to him?"

"No, it's no use. He's angry tonight. Go away, Nicolina. It looks as though we're talking behind his back. That wouldn't be right."

But Don Lucio's mood that evening was disposed toward peace. He had eaten with a good appetite, and had had no trouble digesting his supper; he was satisfied. The only thing he found rather annoying was to hear his wife crying in there.

Finally he got up and went into the bedroom, while Nicolina, who had gone back to her sewing, went pale with fright.

His wife, seated in the shadow beside the boy's cot, looked almost beautiful in the sorrowing abandon of her whole person. Don Lucio felt the desire to embrace her. Already he seemed to feel in his thin arms the soft warm body of his wife, who yielded compliantly to his grasp.

At that moment she had no thought whatever of being compliant. Her mind and heart were completely taken up by her sick child.

Don Lucio gazed at the cot with a kind of repugnance. Ever since he was born, the boy had brought nothing but annoyance to him and anxiety to the women.

"Silly!" he exclaimed, with unaccustomed mildness in his voice. "Do you think your son is about to die?"

Antonietta was startled at hearing her husband's voice. But since she saw he was smiling, she was bold

5

enough to explain, "He can't hold anything down, not even water. And just feel how he's burning."

"I can see you don't know much about it!" replied Don Lucio, without looking at the sick boy. "If your mother were here, she'd tell you how silly you are. Children are as unpredictable as spring weather."

Antonietta felt slightly reassured. Much as he intimidated her, her husband's presence was enough to make all her apprehensions seem minor and unfounded.

But the comfort lasted only as long as Don Lucio's presence. Left alone once more in the semidarkness of the room, she was again gripped by her fears. The boy seemed to be dozing; his delicate little face, white as wax, frightened her. She stared at him sorrowfully, as though hoping by her gaze to transmit vitality to him.

"Alessio, my love . . . Alessiuccio . . ." she called softly, so that she might see him open his eyes. But then it occurred to her that rest would do him good, and she went back to gazing at him in silence. With her entire soul concentrated in her fixed and frightened stare, she forgot about her husband, her daughter, and the late hour. If the house had collapsed around her, she would not have moved but would have gone on gazing at her sick child! No one cared about the little boy, who might seem to be dozing but was actually suffering and unable to rest. He might even die right there in the overwhelming silence, while her husband went on entering his figures on sheets of paper ruled with red and blue lines . . . What would he do, what would he say, if she were to call out to him, "Lucio! Alessiuccio is dead . . ."?

Did he really love Alessio? Of course, he must love him, for he was their first child, and a boy. Of course

. . . But the shadow of doubt, flitting through her mind like a bat in the night, was enough to redouble her maternal love.

The truth was that ever since his birth, Alessio had brought nothing but anxiety. Frail, delicate, quiet, it was as though he walked the earth watched over by death.

Who had spoken these grim words, which only now, when he was so sick, came back to her ears? Certainly they had been spoken for her Alessiuccio . . . She had given him life more than once, and with equal pain. "My God, my God!" she moaned, "how can I ever make him strong and happy and boisterous like other boys?"

Her husband came back, a candle in his hand. "Aren't you in bed yet?" he exclaimed.

"Right away," Antonietta replied. "Don't shine the light in his eyes," she implored him.

Obediently, she undressed and got into bed. But she tried not to fall asleep. At midnight she got up to make Alessio drink, and then twice more to take his temperature.

"Mamma!" the sick boy cried on seeing her. "Is it daylight yet?"

She had got out of bed cautiously and walked barefoot, so as not to wake her husband. Nevertheless Don Lucio was awakened. In the morning he said to her, pointing to the cot, "For as long as he's sick, I'm sleeping out there. I can't afford to go on losing a night's sleep."

Antonietta lowered her eyes in mortification. He was right. A man who works with his brains has need of consideration, and cannot be expected to give up his sleep like a mere woman.

Still, when Don Lucio left the room to go and drink his coffee, she was unable to hold back her tears. She felt a great chill, almost as though she had been left forever alone and abandoned in the semidarkness of the room, its air saturated with the rank odor of fever.

Her sister was calling. She left the boy's bedside so as not to irritate her husband further by making him wait.

Nicolina had got up very early, and after preparing coffee, had swept and tidied the large room, which, perhaps because of its dark draperies and the fact that it gave on the narrow street, received no light until the late morning. Her brother-in-law's clothes, already brushed and folded, lay ready on the divan, and his shoes, well polished, had been placed on a stool so that he wouldn't have to stoop for them. From the kitchen came a strong and pleasant aroma of fresh coffee.

Antonietta gulped down her coffee, and as her sister hurried by with a clean towel on her arm, said urgently, "I'm going back to Alessio, Nicoli'. See to breakfast, would you?"

Nicolina did not reply. Knowing that her sister was unable to think about her household tasks, she had already been taking care of them herself since the previous evening. Don Lucio was washing in the kitchen, rubbing his thin, hairy arms and shaven cheeks with sweet-smelling soap, and then amply rinsing himself. Nicolina waited modestly for him to finish in order to hand him the towel, overcoming the disagreeable impression made on her by those naked male arms. Then she brought him his toothbrush. Finally she remembered that Antonietta combed his hair.

Don Lucio took a seat in front of the closed French window, a dry towel around his neck.

"Let's see how good you are."

Nicolina sprinkled lotion on his sparse tufts of hair, and rubbed lightly with a small sponge until the scalp turned pink. Then she applied the comb.

"Is that all right?"

"That's fine."

"I'm not hurting you?"

"No. Go on."

Nicolina was good at it. She had long been observing and learning every one of her sister's slightest movements as, twice a day, she combed her husband's hair. She now endeavored to do the same, as slowly as possible, without getting impatient, prompted by the fear of displeasing her brother-in-law, who was entrusting his pink bald skull to her inexperienced hands.

"Is that all right?"

"That's fine."

"I'm not hurting you?"

Don Lucio was enjoying his first pleasure of the day. The slow, steady massage did him good; with his shoulders comfortably propped against the low back of the chair, his eyes half-closed, he gave himself up completely to this small voluptuous sensation.

"That's enough," he ordered at a certain point.

Nicolina put away the combs and the little bottle of lotion, and ran to wash herself. Then she dashed upstairs. Carmelina was awake; she dressed her and brushed her hair; she tidied the two rooms with all the liveliness of movement that came naturally to her and which was so displeasing to Don Lucio. She came back downstairs, and while preparing breakfast, resumed once more all the necessary sedateness she had learned to show in waiting on her brother-in-law.

She spread the tablecloth, buttered the white bread (it was made separately, for him alone, with the most expensive flour), and poured the milk, not too hot and not too cold. While he ate—a doctor had advised him to chew each mouthful slowly thirty times—Nicolina did not neglect him for a minute. She went back and forth between the dining room and the kitchen, where other slices of bread were toasting on the fire, she stood ready to butter them, to offer more milk or sugar, and still without overcoming her nagging fear of not satisfying her brother-in-law. Intent on these duties, she refrained from tackling the many other chores that awaited her, or preparing breakfast for herself and Antonietta. Anyway they, being women, were used to getting along with a piece of bread and a little ricotta cheese eaten on the run. She peered at her brother-in-law's face, anxious for his approval. But Don Lucio's scowl was as dark as midnight. He went with slow steps into the bedroom, scuffling his slippers.

Antonietta gazed at him through her tears. "Lucio!" she exclaimed softly. "How does he look to you?"

Don Lucio glanced at the sick boy, who was staring at him with burning, dilated eyes. "He has a cold," he said irritably. "Can't you see his eyes are watering? See that he gets a good sweat."

And he went to get dressed. He couldn't stand scenes with sick people whining and women weeping. What did they want from him? Why did they keep pestering him, following him around with looks so grievous that they seemed only to reproach him? The boy's health was out of his hands! Here he'd eaten a good breakfast and now they wanted to spoil it for him. That was all.

Well, a child's life could hardly be as useful as the

life of a grown man who "works and produces." As his own life, after all. He himself had heart trouble. He was not supposed to get upset. And they insisted on poisoning his existence with the little problems and silly fears with which women muddle their heads. Well, if he were to die, they'd have nothing to eat!

But these thoughts were as unpleasant and inappropriate as the sight of his sick son. Better not to think about it. He touched his legs, his arms; he looked at himself for a long time in the mirror, where his reflection seemed to emerge as from greenish water. He lived, he breathed, he saw. He took a deep breath. Looking at himself in the mirror, he discovered two new white hairs; he pulled them out and discarded them with repugnance. He wasn't so young any more. Perhaps the decay of his body was already beginning, while another creature born of him would survive him. Every day that passed was one more step taken by him toward death, and by the other toward the future. They were moving toward opposite goals. There was no help for it. Such is Nature.

Getting dressed to go out, his gaze rested involuntarily on the cot. Quickly he turned his eyes away. Yes, the other would certainly recover. He had a whole life ahead of him, a fresh new life . . .

Antonietta, mortified, was looking at her husband. She could see he was getting more and more enraged.

He was right to be. She had been neglecting him for several days and perhaps Nicolina had been unable to look after him properly. To gain his pardon, she carefully brushed his jacket and accompanied him to the vestibule, where Nicolina was waiting, holding his light-colored duster with arms outspread. Don Lucio put it on without speaking. At the door he turned, look-

11

ing taller than ever, and said harshly, without addressing himself to either one of the women, "Don't forget to make up my bed in the small sitting room."

Now that they were alone, the two sisters, without acknowledging it, felt a kind of relief. It was as though they breathed more freely in the house, the vast unlighted house.

"How is he?" Nicolina asked.

"Bad, Nicolinedda. I'm scared. What scares me most is not knowing what he has." And since Nicolina was still questioning with her eyes, she added, "He doesn't want to believe how sick he is. Men are all like that. He thinks I'm exaggerating."

"But what about papa, God rest his soul? Remember when Alfonso had meningitis?"

"Papa was one in a million. Men are all like Lucio. Believe me, Nicolinedda, I know. I've had more experience than you."

Nicolina gave a deep sigh. Of course, it couldn't be otherwise.

She went to look in on her nephew. But faced with the grave, intelligent gaze of the sick boy asking for help, she was completely shaken, gripped by a feeling of oppression and dismay. She too felt surrounded in the house by the most relentless solitude. There wasn't a soul on whom they could call for comfort or advice. No one knocked at their door but unknown people, people who asked in humble tones for Don Lucio, while sizing up the women with hostility.

She left the bedroom in order to dispel her feeling of anguish and solitude, and began setting up an iron cot in the small sitting room, while Carmelina, excited by the innovation, skipped around her.

It was essential that Don Lucio not feel he was camping out. So after removing the Oriental rug and the bronze clock under its fragile glass bell, she carried into the sitting room all the little comforts with which he liked to surround himself. Here was the crystal glass receptacle that held his scented soap, sponge, and toothbrush. Here the nice oblong mirror. And the mysterious ebony box, which he always kept locked on top of the chest of drawers. The artificial leather case for his combs. The holder for the steel nail file and little curved scissors. And finally the case with all the things needed for shaving at home every three days. Nicolina had a kind of adoration for all these little objects, which she placed on the furniture in the sitting room. Things that seemed useless, or anyway superfluous ... Her father, God rest his soul, had been so simple! As had her girl friends' brothers in former days. They had all been so different from him!

As she closed the shutters to keep the sun out of the transformed sitting room, it occurred to her that a poor girl like herself, made for hard work, would never dare to sleep in such a beautiful, luxurious room.

Of course, she thought, he's different from all the others. And she regretted her inability to demonstrate sufficient trust in him when she had been alone with Antonietta. If he wasn't alarmed, that was truly a sign that Alessio was in no danger. He knew what needed to be done; he was sure of himself and knew all about life, like someone reading from an open book. One need only have confidence in him, and set one's mind at rest.

And once again she felt the keen sense of gratitude and admiration that seemed to occupy the space separating her poor self from her brother-in-law.

He could have married a rich and educated young lady from the city, and instead he had stooped to look at little Antonietta, who had brought him no other dowry but her trousseau, no other jewels but her virtues as a housewife.

Well, she repeated to herself, lingering as though enraptured in the middle of the darkened room, Antonietta was lucky. Once these little difficulties were over, her sister would go back to savoring the joy of belonging to a man who knew how to guide her, of having a house of her own, children of her own.

Yes, she had been lucky. Almost nothing was lacking for her to be happy.

The story of Antonietta's marriage was very simple.

Don Lucio Carmine had for some years been the administrator, or rather factotum, to Baron Rossi. Every spring he would go to Sant'Agata, where the baron owned houses and lands, to collect the revenues, and would be given hospitality by the town clerk, Don Pasquale Restivo.

The late Don Pasquale had felt such profound gratitude to him that he would have cut off his hands for him.

This is how it happened. The town clerk, hoping to raise money for his daughters' dowries, had had the idea of going into business and had started a factory. But it was like someone setting out on the high seas in a fragile skiff: his slender capital was soon consumed.

Seeing that he had got himself, as the expression goes, into a fix, his wife came up with the name of Don Lucio Carmine.

"He's not rich, but he's doing all right. The very fact

that the baron trusts him so highly shows that he won't tell people about our affairs. They say he lent money to the pharmacist when he went broke from gambling."

Maybe the poor woman was inspired by an angel, maybe by a malicious imp. But who, in the grip of necessity, can tell the difference between good and evil?

Don Pasquale traveled to the city to seek out Don Lucio; he signed promissory notes, offering as security his house and a small piece of land that produced a year's supply of grain. Don Lucio made a special trip to Sant'Agata, with an appraiser friend who evaluated the house and land, and then he put up the money. Coming when it did, it was providential!

Time went swiftly by. Don Pasquale, who was not cut out to be a businessman, continued on his ruinous way with a factory that seemed cursed by the Lord. And one evening, when he least expected it, he was handed a visiting card from Signor "Lucio Maria Carmine, secretary to Baron Rossi, etc., President of the Merchants' Club, etc., Member of the League for Abandoned Children, etc., etc." He was in the village and wished to "point out" that the promissory notes were coming due.

Don Pasquale rushed despairingly to the small hotel where Don Lucio was staying. The latter received him with his usual coolness.

"We'll see," he limited himself to saying, without raising his eyes (at that time he did not yet wear glasses) from several loose sheets of paper scattered on the bed. "We'll see. But as it turns out, I'm overdrawn. I've made sacrifices for you."

"You're right!" moaned the town clerk. "You're ab-

15

solutely right. But just think of my situation as the poor father of a family! You're young, you don't know what it means! The good name of the Restivos is at stake! The shame! And where can I show my face if they take away my house? We haven't been on time. But now we'll pay. You're right. But you won't lose anything. You're dealing with an honest man. I've paid the interest to date . . ."

"And who's talking about interest? You take me for someone who goes in for that sort of thing?" Don Lucio interrupted, raising his voice and chin. "That's what I get for helping people out!"

"I didn't mean to offend you!" explained the town clerk, sighing painfully. "I'm not suggesting anything illegal!"

"We'll see," repeated Don Lucio, who, very tall and frowning, with a wisp of graying hair on one temple, looked older than he actually was. "I'm not such a bad soul. I wouldn't hurt a fly, and my conscience is as clear as a baby's at its mother's breast. But mind you, I've waited far too long and now I'm overdrawn."

He enjoyed hearing himself beseeched and implored by a man already old, who was respected by everyone in the village and now stood bareheaded before him, his trembling hands stretched out as though warding off a danger.

"We'll see." He said nothing more, pretending, with a look of vexation, to go on searching through his papers. "I'll let you know," he added finally.

The town clerk went away, sick at heart.

Every evening when he got home, he would ask, "Has he come? Has he written?"

"He hasn't come, and he hasn't written," his wife

replied. "But don't be alarmed. Between our friends and relatives . . ."

"Yes, our friends and relatives!" exclaimed the town clerk disconsolately. "Making my affairs public! Don't you realize that the poor and the sick get turned away by their relatives?"

"There's always Mastro Don Biasi."

"Mastro Don Biasi? You'd throw me into the clutches of a moneylender? He'd gobble up everything for sure!"

This went on for a whole week. A week that seemed like that of the Crucifixion. Even the children thought about the promissory notes, and mentioned them in whispers when their father wasn't around.

Finally Don Lucio Carmine appeared. He renewed the notes on a long-term basis, and took over the factory himself—that factory that was still being built and had swallowed up all the capital, like a bottomless well. There was nothing to do but accept it. What was done was done. Now it was just a question of paying, with no more thought to ill-advised speculations.

Don Pasquale Restivo returned to life from death. What consoled him most was that, in the midst of such a disaster, his land had not been touched.

"But there's still the danger," said his wife. "The land is there, as security. And if . . ."

The town clerk frowned. But he brightened immediately. Nonsense. He would pay the debt even if it meant eating dry bread.

"Next year," he concluded, "we'll invite him to dinner. He's an honest man."

He spoke of him with respect, almost as though he were the village deputy. "An honest man! Someone else, in his place, would have ruined me. It's true, I got my fingers burned and don't have much left. But never mind. The house and the land are still ours. And I won't let anyone take them away."

His brood of children stood listening, open-mouthed. They were almost afraid of that tall, frowning man who, like God Almighty, was able to produce sunshine or bad weather.

At the time Caterina, the eldest, may have been twenty; next came Antonietta, Nicolina, and their little brothers.

The following year Don Lucio was invited to dinner, on all the days he spent in Sant'Agata. And this business of inviting him to dinner became a habit. When they heard of Don Lucio Carmine's arrival, Donn'Amalia and the girls set to work almost as though it were Easter. They cleaned the whole house, washing even the windows, even the copper door handles, and got out the linen tablecloth with the red and white monogram, so as to receive in proper fashion the guest arriving from the city. Since there was more to eat than usual and many other little novelties as well, his coming always made the town clerk's children happy.

It was only Antonietta who was still overcome by an indefinable sense of fear. This young man who seemed to be getting old before his time, who sat at the table and chewed his food so slowly that it was painful to watch him, who seldom spoke and never laughed, inspired in her such awe as to take her breath away, exactly as though there was suddenly no more air in the sunny little dining room. With time the fear became almost pleasant, almost alluring. Without knowing why, she began looking forward to Don Lucio's visits with a certain impatience. Perhaps she looked forward to them as the only event that came to break the monotony of her domestic existence.

He arrived regularly every spring, in company with the friend and expert who had appraised the Restivo property; he did not come only on behalf of the baron, but also to look after his own interests and see the factory, which was making visible progress and which, once it was finished, he had every intention of selling.

Working in the kitchen garden, behind the little wall that in summer smelled of sunshine, Antonietta thought of Don Lucio and tried to imagine the house where he lived all by himself. But she quickly laughed at herself, to herself, since it seemed stupid to let her thoughts wander around a person who may not even have remembered seeing her. The reserved and taciturn yearly guest had never looked her in the face, nor had he ever spoken to her directly. For him, she was merely one of the daughters of a man who owed him money. Perhaps he was already engaged to a rich, proud young lady in the city.

Little Antonietta was mistaken. Don Lucio, in his brief aloof visits, had observed and scrutinized her. For three years he had accepted the dinner invitations so as not to ruin his digestion with the meals concocted at the inn, and to get to know the town clerk's second daughter better. Nicolina was too young. Caterina exhibited a haughty and unsociable nature, and her expression and rather brusque demeanor gave rise to the fear that she was overly sure of herself and only waiting for the right moment to have her own way.

He liked Antonietta. She was not beautiful, but neither was she plain. She had a pair of brown eyes filled with gentleness. Her dark dress displayed the outline of a body already developed and well formed. Her large rough hands and sturdy wrists were familiar with humble and necessary household chores. He liked her. She seemed to him the true image of woman. He, who dimly remembered his sisters, couldn't abide city girls, who flirt and attend boys' schools. For some time he had been thinking of getting married; now he had even found a girl of the kind that suited him. But he needed to get used to the idea of having to live with Antonietta, and above all, to assure himself that her character was truly meek and docile, made to be molded like fresh clay.

One thing was necessary: to wait until Don Pasquale Restivo had finished paying him (in a short time the interest had exceeded the capital), since business and sentiment do not go well together.

He made up his mind when the time seemed ripe. And so as not to tire himself by making a special trip, he waited until he had to go to Sant'Agata on the baron's behalf. Anyway he was in no hurry to take Antonietta into the vast house where he lived by himself, and where from time to time he brought some humble adoring mistress. It was the fifth year that the town clerk, with unvarying cordiality, had welcomed him as a guest.

He spoke gravely of the girl, from time to time mechanically brushing away, out of his innate love for cleanliness and order, the birdseed that the canaries in the cage were spattering on his knees. The town clerk was enthralled by the scrupulous honesty of this young man who—with a specific emotion—had frequented his house without disturbing Antonietta's peace of mind or taking advantage of his position as creditor.

Antonietta was summoned on the spot. She was in the kitchen garden, shelling a basket of peas and singing with Nicolina. The gay, clear voices of the two sisters reached the dining room. On the stairs her mother took her hand and whispered, "My child, Don Lucio Carmine has come asking to marry you."

Antonietta went pale. Bewildered, she wanted to flee. Her mother drew her gently into the dining room. Don Lucio was standing with his back to the doorway, his tall figure obscuring the whole glass window; the town clerk was pointing out to him some orchards in the distance that long ago had belonged to the Restivo family. They turned. Antonietta stood there on the threshold, her face whiter than wax; she looked around as though seeking help in her crushing dismay.

"You look like a silly goose," said her mother, smiling. "What will Signor Don Lucio think of you?"

They were all embarrassed. Then Don Lucio said, "I hope that Donna Antonietta will consider her answer well."

And he went out. That, too, was the gesture of a gentleman.

But Antonietta felt more deeply troubled than ever, as though they had abandoned her on a deserted road. If the guest had so much as looked into her eyes, if he had spoken one kind word to her, her heart would have opened to joy and love like a flower that blooms when touched by the sun.

What was this great sorrow that oppressed her so? She began to cry softly, her face buried in her apron. The canary kept hopping about its cage and a few millet seeds stayed tangled in her glossy black hair.

21

"It's good for her to unburden herself," said the town clerk. "All girls are like that. Remember, Amalia?"

And Donn'Amalia and Don Pasquale nodded their heads, smiling sweetly like two big overgrown children, remembering those distant days full of the happiness of being young and in love. Wonderful days! Donn'Amalia, too, had cried then, and the others had smiled. And later they had had the portrait made (the one that now hung, yellowed, in the drawing room), she seated, he standing with one hand resting on the back of the armchair, stiff and straight so that it would be a good likeness, while their hearts were beating like drums. Wonderful days! Everything had slowly faded, like the setting summer sun that lingers in the middle of the sea. And they thought that in their children they were reliving this tender past history.

Nicolina, coming up the stairs, found Antonietta with reddened eyes. Loving her sister as she did, she too went pale.

"It's nothing," their mother explained, in a voice that quavered a little. "Don Lucio Carmine has come asking to marry her."

Even Nicolina did not ask if Antonietta had accepted. Delighted, she started to laugh, repeating in a sing-song voice, as though telling the old fairy tale to a child: "Here comes Bluebeard! Will you give me the nicest of your sisters?"

"Oh, shut up!" cried Caterina, who had not said a word. "You're always making jokes at the wrong moment. Well, what's so funny now? Help me set the table."

It pained Caterina that her sister should get married. Wasn't life beautiful and pleasant enough as it was, with all of them staying together, joined like grapes in a single bunch? Now one of them was to leave the tranquil house and follow a strange man. She wanted to ask: Do you like him? Will you really marry him? But she said nothing. She mustn't, by her words, come between her sister and her fate.

For the same reason perhaps, everyone avoided speaking of the "new situation." And the morning passed like any other, amid the heightened preparations for the guest's dinner. That evening, at dinner, Don Lucio Carmine without asking for Antonietta's well-considered answer, presented her with a ring that looked extraordinarily beautiful and expensive. And after his departure, things returned to normal.

The big events were the future bride's trousseau and the visits of her girl friends, who came to congratulate her and satisfy their curiosity. They all envied the girl; many took a spiteful pleasure in whispering that this was an arranged marriage. The town clerk was handing his daughter over to a stranger, without first finding out anything about him, in exchange for the settlement of certain promissory notes. For a while they talked of nothing else, then they stopped talking about it, as happens with any piece of news that causes a sensation.

Antonietta did not overcome the awe that her fiancé inspired in her. He came two or three more times during the year, in order to "get to know" her and offer advice about the trousseau, urging them not to incur needless expenses, foolish expenses. Antonietta did not "get to know" him. She became more and more convinced that she was a poor creature who would never be at ease with this wise, taciturn man, and never get him to love her. Why choose me? she wondered, dismayed. And she felt as though she were dragging an intolerable burden.

On the eve of the wedding, she was bold enough to ask a great favor of her fiancé, a "kindness," as she called it. So as not to be alone in the new house, she would like to take Nicolina along, at least for the first days.

"She's still a child, you could say. She won't be any trouble."

Of course, how could she be any trouble? Don Lucio was used to seeing Nicolina at Antonietta's side, gay and constant witness of their brief conversations as an engaged couple, and he agreed at once.

So Nicolina packed her things in her trunk (one of those small painted green boxes that come from Palermo full of cakes); she had her traveling bag and her duster. She was happy to be going to a city and expressed her happiness so vivaciously that you would have thought she was the bride.

"A bride with no ring and no groom," she told her girl friends, laughing.

When she came down the stairs, preceded by the porter with the green box on his shoulders, she was quivering impatiently, like a bird on its first flight. She was leaving her home and her mother without a shadow of regret. Her exuberant youth was thirsting to see new things. And besides, she knew she would soon be back.

It had been decided that she would stay with her sister no more than a month or six weeks. But Antonietta wanted to postpone her departure, and her husband gave in.

Antonietta could not get used to the idea of being alone by letting her young sister leave. In her husband's presence she did not dare to have wishes, or hopes. She was a poor thing with no will of her own. If it had been her husband's whim to order her, "Jump out the window!" she would have jumped headlong, worse than a blind woman. When he said to her, "I'm busy," she walked on tiptoe, spoke in signs to Nicolina, or even left the rooms from which her husband might hear some noise that would disturb him. When he called her, she came running immediately. And when he wanted her, she leaned on his chest with total and passive devotion.

She was not happy. There was a chill in her heart that made joy impossible. Whenever she found herself alone for a few moments in the large, silent downstairs rooms, she felt restless, lost, and ran to look for Nicolina. She thought with terror of the day when Nicolina would have to leave her forever.

They would sit and sew together on the balcony overlooking the narrow street, chatting like two good friends. Avoiding any mention of Don Lucio, they spoke seldom of the present and often of the past, the uniform past that now appeared in their memories with beautiful things never seen, never felt "back then." They spoke of it as of a treasure forever lost. And yet they never complained. The sadness that was blighting their young hearts did not have a specific cause. It was in the air they breathed: the whole house was imbued with it, the vast and isolated house where every noise reverberated deeply, rising up from the depths of the dark street, where sometimes they saw a wretched woman, known as the Redhead, crouching on the worn steps of her house. The first floor, with two large iron balconies whose windows were always closed, looked uninhabited. But sometimes a pale woman dressed in black came out on the balcony to water a scrubby, wilted geranium. She was a widow, still young, who lived with her paralytic father.

"You don't find many houses like this in the city," Don Lucio had boasted. "Once the door is closed, we need have nothing more to do with the neighbors."

They had a confused, painful impression of the city, which they had barely glimpsed. The city (full of crowded streets where we cling to Don Lucio so as not to get lost, full of people whom we perhaps will never meet, who will never give us a joyful smile . . .), the city was still remote, unknown, almost frightening.

Nicolina was losing her good healthy color, and they kept talking about her departure. But Antonietta was unable to make the break.

When the telegram arrived announcing the town clerk's sudden death, Nicolina's departure became quite out of the question. Don Lucio allowed them to go and visit their mother. And for their return, it was taken for granted that Nicolina would follow her married sister, and this time she cried bitterly because she knew she was going to the dark house on the narrow street not to please the wife, but to accept the generous hospitality of her brother-in-law.

The little red house in Sant'Agata, with its two slender poplars in back, closed its shutters. The widow confined her existence to two rooms, and posted outside on the gate a placard reading: "To let—small apartment with kitchen." The idea of the "to let" sign came from Don Lucio, with his city habits. But it was pointless, of course, since everyone knew the house was for rent. Some pieces of furniture were stored in the attic, others were left here and there in the emptied rooms. The family split up and disbanded. An uncle in San Fratello took Alfonso. The paternal grandfather assumed responsibility for Antonio.

Caterina said: "When Antonietta went away it brought us bad luck. That's what happens when the first stone falls. Soon the whole wall crumbles and collapses."

Don Lucio gave assurances that he would see to the future of the orphan girl Nicolina, and would not forget the widow. In the village they admired him, and felt sorry for him. Willingly or not, he'd made a bad marriage! Now he had a whole family on his hands! As they left the house to return to the city, the two women in front, dressed in black, looking back with sobs at the gate with the "to let" sign, he walking behind, stiff as a ramrod, many people came up to shake his hand.

The two sisters, finding themselves back in the house in the city as though after a bad dream, became more closely attached to each other than ever. Their gratitude to Don Lucio was boundless. Thinking of the poor scattered little family, they understood what it meant to have a large comfortable home and a full larder, and above all to be able to rely on a man who provides for the present and the future. He was not only Antonietta's husband, but a kind of benefactor. In the deep prostration into which their recent loss had thrown them, they wanted somehow to repay him.

Nicolina asked that the servant, an old woman who performed the heavier chores and did the laundry, be let go. She was ashamed to be a burden to her brother-

27

in-law. And since by then Antonietta was pregnant for the first time and needed special care, she took on all the housework herself.

With the birth of Alessio—a tiny, sickly baby, who seemed to be molded of the suffering of those months of mourning and of the melancholy that emanated from the house—Nicolina no longer had any respite.

"Nicolina, the hot water!"

"Nicolina, Lucio will be back any minute and supper isn't ready!" Antonietta would call.

And Don Lucio would order: "Antonietta, tell Nicolina to fill my pipe. Tell Nicolina to polish my shoes and bring them to me."

And Nicolina, anxious to please, seemed to be all over the place at once, in her effort to get everything done and satisfy everyone. She was skinny, but strong. She seemed made of fine steel. Many times, Antonietta, nursing the baby or changing his diapers, would urge her, "Run and see if Lucio needs me for anything!"

At first Don Lucio was annoyed at having her always underfoot, and grumbled about the kid sister who was stealing his wife's attentions from him. Her radiant young eyes and lively movements did not inspire his confidence. Then gradually he got used to it, since the girl changed in his presence and in serving him became as silent and serious as Antonietta.

In time, adding it all up, Don Lucio was glad he had played the benefactor: Nicolina was worth more than a servant, since to a servant he had to pay wages and all Nicolina cost him was a little food and an occasional dress.

Fortunately, neither she nor Antonietta needed very

many dresses and shoes. They had gone out barely three or four times. With the death of their father, they shut themselves in out of necessity. Mourning, which one wears for years and years, is an economical thing. Then nursing the baby . . . Finally Antonietta began to suffer again, as when she had been pregnant with Alessio.

Such, however, are the lives of all wives.

Therefore they never spoke of going out for a breath of fresh air. And Don Lucio, for his part, did his best to see that no such wish arose. Too much fuss and bother! They'd need a servant to carry the child, who still didn't walk, and a black shawl for Antonietta, who couldn't show herself in public in her condition. Foolish expenses, useless expenses! And besides, he'd have to alter his comfortable habits. No more after-dinner smoke, no more lemonade to be sipped unhurriedly. Nothing, nothing. Better that life should run like clockwork, while women remained in their place. Besides— he assured himself to remove any qualms—nuns do all right in their cloister and live long lives. Women don't waste energy.

It was after having ruminated these things, drowsing after his smoke at the end of supper, that he would often conclude, stretching his arms a little:

"Yes! Happiness consists of habit!"

And he looked at the two sisters, who were engrossed in their sewing by the light of the lamp (he, Don Lucio, used oil lamps, because paraffin and gas irritate the eyes), to see if they approved.

They expressed their approval by nodding their heads, since whatever he said could not be anything but true and proper. But they hadn't heard his remark.

All evening they had been thinking silently and intently of the red house with the "to let" sign, and the little family scattered here and there.

Alessio was getting worse. Don Lucio felt vaguely responsible for the sick boy's life.

"We ought to call a doctor," Antonietta said timidly.

"Yes, a doctor . . ." Nicolina chimed in softly.

The mere thought of a strange man entering his house, and gaining the trust and gratitude of his wife, made him profoundly uneasy.

But the boy was getting worse. And Don Lucio, no longer able to stand the sniveling of his womenfolk, who seemed almost to be taxing him with indifference, went in person one evening to the nearest pharmacy, to see if he could find a doctor.

While the mother and aunt, their eyes and noses red, waited anxiously, following every gesture of the doctor, who was examining the patient in silence, he too waited, with the rather proud air of someone who has sacrificed himself in the performance of his duty. He seemed to say, "I've done all I can." And indeed his conscience was clear. Alessio could even die now, if that was to be his fate, and the two women would no longer have any cause to blame him.

It was typhus. For some fifty days Antonietta did not leave the bedroom. She would drink a raw egg, a cup of broth, to stay on her feet. She took no interest in anything or anybody. She was completely wrapped up in her sick boy, his countless needs, his long periods of exhaustion, his fleeting moments of improvement.

Don Lucio, who had a mortal fear of contagion, went on sleeping and eating alone.

The whole burden of the house fell on Nicolina.

From the time she got up—and she got up while it was still dark—until late at night, she did not allow herself a moment's rest. She had to do all the big and little chores, iron, cook, and see to everything. Her main concern was to spare her brother-in-law as much as possible the consequences of this cursed sickness. At mealtimes she remained on her feet, even when her legs trembled from fatigue, ready to change his plate (in order to bring him his food piping hot the way he liked it, she heated the plate over the stove), to pour him something to drink, to peel his fruit. Peeling fruit was the most delicate task. Antonietta had never been able to skin an orange so well, first removing the rind, then with a penknife stripping away every last bit of the white inner skin, every filament, without puncturing it! Pears and apples, carefully peeled and cut in pieces, one piece already stuck on the little silver fork . . .

To sit down at the table with her brother-in-law when Antonietta was not there seemed to her a breach of manners. Later, however, she would have a bite to eat in the kitchen, along with Carmelina who waited like a kitten, hoping her aunt would bring back a few scraps of the choice dishes specially prepared for the master of the house. After clearing the table, she filled his pipe. She fixed his lemonade. She put her niece to bed (ever since Alessio had been sick, the little girl slept upstairs on a cot next to her own). Then she waited, huddled in a corner, her eyelids heavy and burning from drowsiness. And the time passed more slowly, the hours seemed to drag, the deep silence broken only by the quiet ticking of the clock and the muted smacking of Don Lucio's lips as he sucked placidly on his

31

pipe. In her drowsiness she thought confusedly that the slow ticking marked the footsteps of time, which goes on and on with no pause and no return.

She waited for her brother-in-law to put aside his pipe and ask for the papers from the shelf. Then he would say, without looking at her:

"You can go to bed, if you're sleepy."

She went to the bedroom to say goodnight to Antonietta. She saw her, by the subdued green light from the lamp, pale, unkempt, and grieving as she watched over the sick boy.

"I'm going to bed. Do you need me for anything?"

Patient and resigned, she tidied the bedroom, and helped her sister to remake the bed, slowly so as not to disturb the boy. At last she climbed the wooden stairs, finally free. She undressed hurriedly, blew out the lamp, and let herself fall heavily on the bed.

Some nights she had trouble falling asleep. She felt a tingling in her whole body, a great wish to cry, to close her eyes and not wake up again. It was certainly the lowest point of exhaustion.

With Alessio's recovery, Nicolina felt she had awakened from a nightmare. She caught herself singing sometimes, when she was by herself, as though she were back in the carefree times of Sant'Agata.

The small sitting room was cleared and put back in order. The windows were thrown open again. Alessio and Carmelina, who herself had got quite run-down, went out two or three times with their father. But since Don Lucio was unwilling to go out in the heat of the day, and the cool evening air was not good for the convalescent, there was no more talk about taking walks.

Besides, with the reopening of the schools, the children would soon be going out every day.

Things returned to normal. But Nicolina was still the one to wait on her brother-in-law. When Antonietta, summoned by her husband, came running, he would say, "If you're busy, send your sister."

And Antonietta would send Nicolina.

"For some things you're better than I!" she exclaimed cheerfully. She was glad to be relieved of a great number of the wearisome tasks she had had to perform for Don Lucio. Nicolina—lucky girl!—was at the age when you did things to the letter. It made Antonietta laugh, observing the trepidation with which she approached her brother-in-law to refill his pipe, the meticulousness with which she peeled his fruit and prepared his evening lemonade.

"Nicolina is better than you!" Don Lucio said, in good-humored tones.

"And I'm not surprised!" Antonietta exclaimed, smiling. "If she had as many worries as I do!"

"But before . . ."

"Before it was a different matter, of course."

He just won't believe, thought Antonietta to justify herself, that the mother of a family can't always be fussing over her husband as though he were a babe in arms! She would begin combing his hair calmly enough, but after ten minutes she regretted wasting time and her hand became nervous and impatient.

But Nicolina's nimble hands worked automatically. She drew the comb again and again over the thinning hair that had been sprinkled with lotion, over the nearly bald and reddish scalp, slowly, slowly, taking her time, while Don Lucio, his pipe between his lips,

33

yielded to the voluptuous sensation of the massage, closing his eyes like a cat being stroked when the comb traveled all the way down the nape of his neck. Sometimes he even forgot that a person standing behind him might get tired. Meanwhile Nicolina's hand remained light and steady.

Don Lucio also helped his wife's family. He administered the small plot of land. When Antonio had come to the city to take the final examination for his technical-school diploma, he had given him hospitality. And three times he had sent gifts of money to the widow.

"Write your mother," he said on one occasion, showing Antonietta the sealed letter, "that I do whatever is humanly possible, for her and the rest of you." And he added: "Tell her to let me know exactly how she spends my money. Common sense is not her strong point."

And Antonietta was troubled for a while before writing, not knowing how to express her husband's wishes without offending her mother. Finally, with Nicolina's help, she composed the letter. Someone who didn't know him might misjudge him and think he was stingy . . . But instead . . .

The gift, accompanied by Antonietta's loving words, which did little to mitigate the severity of Don Lucio's demand, acquired a double value.

"It's all right," the widow insisted, trying to convince her children, who kept grumbling about it. "I can't expect him to treat me like your poor father, God rest his soul. For him, I'm an outsider. He already does too much. As long as Antonietta is happy, what do I matter?"

And she gave an accounting of the money:

"Dearest son-in-law. Out of the fifty lire you sent with your much appreciated insured letter, I paid the shoemaker the twenty lire I owed him. I also gave twenty-five lire on account to the weaver, who had just set up her loom to do sheets. With the other five lire I bought some twill to make aprons for Caterina and me, since we needed them."

Don Lucio, putting on his glasses, read and re-read several times this poor little letter edged in black, while Antonietta waited fearfully, like a child who knows she deserves to be punished.

"That's women for you," Don Lucio said finally. "Why go into debt for shoes? Why have the loom set up when you can't afford it? In less than no time she's spent it all to the last penny. I figured as much. I knew it wouldn't make any difference whether I sent money to Sant'Agata or threw it out the window."

Antonietta held her breath. Don Lucio slowly folded the letter and went to put it in the drawer of the desk, quite satisfied: he had been obeyed by his mother-in-law and made his wife feel the value of his gift.

The administration of Baron Rossi's property, which Don Lucio exercised along with the notary Marullo (two bailiffs took care of the land), occupied a good deal of his time. The extremely wealthy baron also owned magnificent buildings in the city.

Don Lucio collected the rents, negotiated leases, and assumed obligations to make repairs. And he was so economical, and became so visibly irritated when a house stood vacant or when they sent for him to show him some serious damage, that it was as though he were losing his own money. Houses and buildings that in the old baron's time had remained closed and abandoned now all produced income. By his continual proofs of interest and activity, Don Lucio gradually gained Baron Rossi's complete trust. Every spring he made a short trip to collect payments or renew leases in the villages, and he proved inexorable with those who did not turn out to be "in order." Willingly, if only to be able to present the accounts to the baron without gaps or deficits, he lent money to insolvent individuals in arrears. Thus, without having been aware of it, he soon found he had put his own funds in circulation. With time, it came to be known. How did people find out? And in the city too, they began to come to him, secretly. The wives of poor clerks, and widows living on pensions, came seeking him at home, or waited for him in the downstairs vestibule as soon as they learned he did not care to receive borrowers, happy to be dealing with a "gentleman" who would not publicize their misfortunes nor take advantage of them for so much as a penny. As pledges they offered him their jewelry, which he concealed in the mysterious ebony box.

In talking to his wife, he never alluded to his little speculations, though he would have liked to show her how much the comfort by which she was surrounded cost him. He was convinced, completely convinced, that he was doing a legitimate business (after all, it boiled down to the fact that he was helping some poor unfortunate souls out of a tight corner, when they would otherwise end up in the clutches of a money-lender). But he was afraid that Antonietta and Nicolina might not understand that the work he did on his own was almost as honest as what he did for the baron.

Evenings he had them bring the briefcase—which the women never even thought of opening—to the table and spent an hour or so going over three or four ledgers: here he entered "credits" and there "debits," here he wrote closely and evenly in a blue column headed *pro memoria*, there he filled a red column with figures under the day's date. Everything was in good order in his papers, as in all his things.

Yes, indeed, all his things! He had a special bracket to hold his pipe, tobacco, and matches, a box in which to keep new shoes (he had all kinds: high boots, low boots, gaiters . . .), and one for old shoes as well. In addition there was a round box for collars, a rectangular one for neckties, a shelf for papers, a little cupboard for keys. The largest boxes were lined up in a small room. Nicolina, dusting the rooms each morning, devoted a good quarter of an hour to "Lucio's little room," where things were so well arranged that if in the middle of the night he had had to look for something, he would have found it in the dark without fail in this or that box, this or that spot.

Just as he kept his accounts and personal articles in order, Don Lucio kept his habits systematic. Life too was divided—like his little room and his ledgers—into several parts, each containing an activity, a habit, a need. For him there were no dark or uncertain sides to the future. Everything was methodically fixed, everything foreseen.

Sometimes, smoking his long pipe (short pipes are harmful to one's health), he was assailed by the troubled memory of a childhood spent in poverty, unloved, the prey of solitude and the indifference of the old grandfather who had raised him. Yes, he had suffered much, and he knew he had the right to whatever comfort and prosperity he had managed to acquire!

But then a shadow would pass amid the beautiful and easy expectations: it was the dark shadow of death—death, which could seize him from one moment to the next, nailing him forever to the very armchair where he was placidly reclining. He went pale, letting the pipe between his lips go out, terrified at the thought of not being able to enjoy the easy life he had created so astutely, the easy comfortable life he had dreamed of in his bitter hours of desolate poverty, when numb, hungry, and embittered, he had watched rich men go by in fur coats and expensive plush gloves.

He was sick. When he put his open hand on his chest, he could feel his irregular heartbeat. The privations, uncertainties, and struggles of the past had weakened that fragile organ that no doctor can heal.

Now both his apprehensions and his memories hurt him, making him nervous and upset. But he would call his wife or sister-in-law, or put up with his children, if only to hear his own voice, speaking to them about some trifling matter.

Now that Alessio had resumed his studies and Carmelina, too, had gone back to school with the nuns, there was plenty of free time after dinner.

Nicolina would take her workbasket (soft baby clothes, flimsy little chemises a few inches in length . . .), and sit outside on the balcony.

Antonietta was bustling about: she rearranged the linen closet and put away the summer clothes, the things that were too light. She was pregnant again. Each time it happened, she would go over the whole house, from top to bottom, with her own hands, and go to confession in the nearby church, as though about to leave on a long journey.

"Well, isn't it as if I was going away?" she said softly. "I have to say goodbye to things, and to all of you. How can I be sure I'll ever open these chests again, or touch any of these things with my own hands? Then you'll say, 'Antonietta was a bad, untidy housewife.' "

Nicolina sewed rather reluctantly. The last swallows passed in flocks in the sky, and seemed to screech goodbye to the places they had to abandon. The roofs shone in the fiery reflection of the sun. A pigeon perched motionless on the cornice like a big bronze bird. There was an almost springlike warmth in the air, a vast hum composed of a myriad of broken and distant voices, of confused sounds. It was the summer slowly fading, a little more each day. From the street rose the whining cries of the Redhead, who had been beaten and kicked out by her lover. She had thrown herself prostrate on the doorstep, and a barefooted urchin, his little shirt scarcely covering his stomach, stood looking at her from a distance. Nicolina, too, looked at her for a moment, more in surprise than pity. She was dirty, filthy, disheveled. Why did she go on suffering and not run away, not free herself from the chain that kept her tied to that locked door? Nicolina blushed, thinking that behind the door must be the lover, the man who had beaten her and would later allow her to come back in, as always. The lover . . . With her lips, she repeated the seductive word to herself.

But was that love?

She frowned, once more looking unwillingly at the Redhead. So even the image of love could sometimes be disgusting. She thought of Caterina, who did not want to get married. Now she understood why. Many women, like Caterina, feel repugnance toward love, without even knowing what it is. Such is life . . .

She resumed her work. The widow had come out on her balcony to hang a faded yellowish blanket, and lingered to pluck a few dry leaves from the geranium that bloomed without sunlight. Her two bands of hair, black as her mourning bodice, imparted marble reflections to her face. She went back inside, leaving the blanket hanging. That yellow color against the black railing also looked sad.

The twilight reddened the sky, the roofs, and the narrow street. Then suddenly the vivid light vanished completely in the violet air.

Nicolina went inside. There was a great silence in the vast house. The children had lighted the lamp and were doing their homework.

"The three king-doms of na-ture. . ." Carmelina read, moving her finger across the page.

"Please!" Alessio interrupted her. "You're disturbing me! Read to yourself."

No one needed her. Still she went into the bedroom. Maybe Antonietta wanted her for something. Her habit of waiting on others did not allow her to enjoy an hour of complete rest.

Husband and wife were sitting beside the closed window. Don Lucio was smoking and had his arm around Antonietta's waist. This time he was unusually happy about his wife's pregnancy: it seemed to him a sign of youth reborn.

They were speaking in low voices. Nicolina remained on the threshold, not daring to enter and sorry to have to turn back. Her pale delicate face colored fleetingly. With an anxiety half angry, half sorrowing, she wondered what they could possibly be saying to each other in all that peace and quiet.

She went back to the terrace, now white in the moonlight, her throat gripped by a great wish to cry. No one needed her.

She was here to contemplate her sister's happiness. Yes, Antonietta was happy. . . Once again she had a vision of her sister as a bride, in the early days. Days already remote, which she relived intensely in a flash. She remembered many things, as fleeting and ungraspable as the fragments of dreams, certain looks exchanged between husband and wife, a languid and bewildered tone of voice, certain ways of smiling, and she started as though "they" suddenly stood in front of her like "then." Again she saw Antonietta emerging from her bedroom with a rather abandoned look of fatigue. It had made no impression on her "then"; it was like someone who reads without understanding, and then upon re-reading, every word becomes alive and full of meaning. Now here was Antonietta again moving slowly through the rooms, while Don Lucio insisted she take care of herself:

"Let Nicolina do it. Don't overexert yourself."

Yes, the heavy work was left to her, as to a humble paid servant. And was this how her life would always be spent? Always?

But little by little the bitterness faded from her heart. She gazed for a long time at her rough red hands. Who could say whether she would ever sew baby clothes for a child of her own? She blushed deeply, as though someone were standing in front of her and had been able to hear the unfinished thoughts floating in her mind like the thin light clouds that at moments veiled the moon in the sky. Then she stopped thinking altogether. She lost herself completely in a tumult of sensations full of emotion and joy. She felt as though she were sleeping and waking, waking and sleeping.

A calm starlight rained down from the sky and the house in the shadows no longer seemed so sad. An almost anguished tenderness, a need to be loved, and to love someone, choked her heart.

Antonietta was calling: "Nicolina! Nicolina! Alessio, where's your aunt?"

She got up. Don Lucio was sitting at the table. Carmelina was stringing beads and Alessio was reading.

She had forgotten the lemonade. She prepared it and brought it on the blue saucer. As she set it down next to the inkwell, she looked at her brother-in-law, furtively and full of curiosity. How could he make her sister happy?

She hoped he would raise his eyes from the ledgers, thinking she might catch in his gaze an expression of kindness. He couldn't always be so rigid, so cold and severe, when he was alone with Antonietta!

But Don Lucio did not lift his head. "Fill my pipe," he ordered curtly.

Oh yes, the pipe. She was forgetting everything! Chagrined, she obeyed at once.

Why should he look at her anyway? What did she represent in her brother-in-law's life? A poor girl being supported out of charity, nothing more. Having come into the house while still a child, wasn't she a little like Alessio, like Carmelina? She would have been so grateful to him for a kind word! It says in the Gospels that man does not live by bread alone.

She went back to the terrace to empty the bowl of the pipe. The evening was calm and luminous. She thought of the quiet walks she used to take at that hour in Sant'Agata, arm-in-arm with a girl friend. What had they chatted about with so much pleasure? About everything and nothing . . . Again she saw the little house full of gaiety and love. Now she was alone.

Yes, she was alone. Antonietta seemed to be moving away from her, more every day. She lived in another world. The good times were gone when they had both been young girls, and had laughed and cried and laughed again with equal ease over every little thing that happened, happy or sad.

"What are you reading that's so interesting?" Don Lucio was asking.

"Look, papa."

Don Lucio looked with visible disapproval at the book, which the boy had handed to him open. He leafed through it, and closed it with a snap.

"I don't like you cluttering up your mind with cheap novels."

"It's not a cheap novel, papa," Alessio replied timidly. "It's by Foscolo. *Iacopo Ortis* by Foscolo."

"It's still a novel. I forbid you to read it. Who gave it to you?"

"Rossi."

"Take it back to him tomorrow. You're too young for it."

"But he's just my age and—"

"That has nothing to do with it. I forbid you, that's

all. Shame on you! A boy who's still in elementary school!"

Alessio got up, his eyes shining with tears. Nicolina whispered to him, "Don't be upset. Papa is right."

"No . . ." said Alessio with a shake of his head, and left the room.

Nicolina brought the pipe to her brother-in-law. He was once again immersed in his papers, frowning but calm. How could Alessio rebel against him in his heart? He was a man who never made a mistake, who knew right from wrong. One could only have faith in him, as in the sailor who steers the boat on the open sea. It's so good to have faith in someone . . . And again her heart swelled with boundless admiration for her brother-in-law.

"Here's your pipe," she said meekly. Once more she waited for him to raise his head, in the hope of catching an expression of benevolence in his eyes. Somewhat distressed and humiliated, she sat down next to her sister. She felt a great need to talk, to move, to hear others talking.

And was this how her life would always be spent? Always? Like one of these silent, heavy, everlasting evenings? There are times in one's youth when the soul is so weak that it cannot bear solitude. And solitude seems like a visible creature, a nightmare creature that squeezes the heart in its two open hands.

"Look at the little baby bonnet, Lucio!" said Antonietta.

"Good girl," replied Don Lucio, smiling.

It was Nicolina who had sewn the baby bonnet, all by herself. Thus all her work went unrecognized and unrewarded, as though traced in sand. For the first time, she felt a spiteful tinge of jealousy, a stab of rancor toward her sister. Yes, yes, her heart repeated with a muffled and tumultuous beat, as silence returned solemnly to the room, yes, you envy your sister.

"There's a visitor in the parlor!" Alessio announced, running into the kitchen, where Nicolina was skimming the broth.

"A visitor? It must be someone who's come to see your papa."

"No, no, it's really a visitor. He asked for mamma too."

"You don't mean it!"

"There, he's leaving."

"So run and see who he is."

"I don't dare, Aunt Nicoli'. It's a gentleman with gold spectacles, that's for sure. But here comes papa. Don't tell him anything, Aunt Nicoli'. . ."

"I'll go," Carmelina offered. "I'll hide and peek."

"Don't bother," Alessio replied. "He's gone. Here comes papa."

Don Lucio came into the dining room. In the doorway, he changed his mind and went into the bedroom. He could see that Antonietta was anxious to speak to him and was afraid she would do so in Nicolina's presence. Antonietta followed him, her eyes bright with joy and impatience, but seeing him scowl, she lost heart.

"He's become a good-looking man," she finally exclaimed.

"What? With that stupid face?" replied Don Lucio irritably.

"He's intelligent. You must have made him uneasy.

45

He was talking to you about Nicolina when you made a sign to me to leave . . ."

Her husband stared at her. After a silence, he said, "Yes, about your sister. But I gave him the answer he deserved. He'll think twice about setting foot in my house again."

Antonietta went pale. "What have you done, Lucio?" she stammered. "He's a decent man. He knows us . . . Papa, God rest his soul, set great store by him . . . He has a good position . . . And besides," she exclaimed sorrowfully, lowering her voice, "it was her chance, poor girl—"

"You like him?" Don Lucio interrupted in ironical tones. "You want to give him your sister? Have I done the wrong thing? I beg your pardon on bended knee. I'll run after him and call him back. I'll run . . . I had no idea that you wanted to get rid of your sister by throwing her into the arms of the first man who comes along . . . That's what I get . . ." he resumed harshly after a new and heavier silence. "That's what I get for wearing out my life on your account! To have to put up with being scolded! To listen to your ingratitude!

"Yes, you accuse me," he went on, while Antonietta kept shaking her head and sobbing. "You have the nerve to judge me according to your own shortsighted views. I know what I'm doing. Your sister isn't a poor country girl any more, an orphan with no dowry and no future! She'll make a good match, worthy of the sister-in-law of Don Lucio Carmine."

His voice became calmer. Antonietta, contrite and humiliated, started to leave the room, but he called her back. "Don't take it into your head to tell your sister about this! Girls start imagining all kinds of things!"

For the rest of the day, he did not go out of the house, not even in the afternoon, and he had them tell a woman who came to see him that he wasn't home. He kept an eye on Antonietta, fearing she might tell the story to her sister.

But Antonietta was not about to disobey him. Toward evening she went to throw herself on the bed, assailed by labor pains. Don Lucio sighed with relief. He sent Alessio running with a note for Donna Filomena Zuppola, and hovered anxiously over his wife. He was almost glad that she was suffering so much, and thereby forgetting the little incident of the morning. He ordered Nicolina to take the children and go upstairs.

"It's none of your business. Go to bed, all three of you."

Nicolina obeyed without reply. Twice before she had been fearful, but not to this extent. Then "it" had happened during the day, and she had still been ignorant of the danger to which her sister was exposed.

"Go to sleep," she repeated, tucking in the boy, who kept questioning her with his eyes. "It's nothing. It will all be over soon."

Carmelina was already asleep.

She did not go to bed. She was restless, agitated; she expected to be called from one moment to the next. She went to the head of the stairs and cocked an ear. The door down below was closed. There was a great silence. At one moment she heard a mournful groan. Who was groaning like that? It couldn't be Antonietta. Maybe the voice came from outside, from the· street. She went back and sat down beside Carmelina's bed, but got up immediately, wringing her hands so as not to cry out. Time was slow, endless, implacable. God, my God, she murmured without moving her lips, get this torture over with.

Again she cocked an ear. Still she heard nothing. Silence weighed on the house, but a new silence, like that of a man who sits watching and thinking in the night.

Once more she heard the ominous words: "Well, isn't it as if I was going away?"

She asked God's pardon for the touch of jealousy that had poisoned her heart a few evenings before. No, her poor sister was not happy. She pictured her in the worst moments: in that bed of pain, or beside the sick Alessio, or under the harsh gaze of her husband. She had done nothing but suffer and she, Nicolina, had not understood. In the agitation that now gripped her, her envy and the malicious feelings she had entertained seemed to her monstrous and unforgivable.

Her sister was alone, alone in the eternal night, alone with her torment. "My God," she moaned aloud, "how awful life is!"

Thus passed the night. Her spirit quivered like a strung bow. The clear light of dawn was framed in the window. The lamp guttered and went out.

She listened again. She heard the hearty voice of Donna Filomena, then Don Lucio's. What were they saying?

She heard a door slam.

She ought to go and help her, not leave her alone . . .

What remorse she would feel if Antonietta . . .

Yes, it must all be over, she thought with terror. Resolutely she went downstairs. At the foot of the stairs she found her brother-in-law. Through the open door, she heard the feeble cry of a baby, a cry that sounded like bleating, with nothing human about it.

"Where are you going, Nicolina?" Don Lucio asked. And he added, "Yes, thank God it's over. It's another girl. I was just coming to tell you. Go back to your room. I'll call you. Keep the children with you. But stop trembling like that. You'll get sick."

This subdued, almost melancholy tone of voice soothed her.

He was sincerely moved. The tragic simplicity of *what had happened* had left him with a sense of awe. At that moment, so full of mystery and anguish, his heart seemed freed of selfishness and open to a feeling of sympathy—as painful as it was fleeting—for those who suffered.

"Yes, dear Nicolina, sometimes life and death come into a house together when two new eyes are opening!"

He put his arm lightly around her waist and propelled her gently toward the stairs.

Nicolina went upstairs slowly. "My God!" she moaned again, "how awful life is!"

Why is anyone born? Who had wanted that little bawling creature? The vigil, the agitation, the anxious waiting, and then her brother-in-law's voice, veiled in unusual tenderness, a whole combination of sensations and emotions had taken away her strength. She collapsed at the foot of the bed and wept. She lost consciousness. When she came to, she saw Alessio holding a glass of water in his hand. He was pale and frightened. Perhaps he too hadn't slept.

"Aunt Nicoli'," he exclaimed, somewhat reassured, having been unable to get his aunt to drink the water, "I called and called, but no one answered. I think papa has gone to bed, too."

Carmelina was still asleep. "Wait here, Alessio," said Nicolina.

She tiptoed downstairs. Donna Filomena's black shawl was no longer on the clothes rack. Cautiously she pushed open the bedroom door. Don Lucio, snoring loudly, was sleeping on the cot. In the large bed, Antonietta, without a drop of blood in her veins, seemed to be dozing. Hearing the slight noise, she opened her eyes. Nicolina knelt beside her.

"My poor sister," Antonietta whispered. "I thought I'd never see you again, and I felt terrible because I hadn't asked you to look after my babies. But you wouldn't have abandoned them, I'm sure you wouldn't have. What are they doing right now?"

"Carmelina is asleep. Alessio is up. Do you want to see him?"

"No, poor Lucio is resting. Later. Later." Exhausted, she fell silent.

On the other side of the bed, wrapped in fine linen and covered with a veil, the "other one" also slept, her little fists closed. Nicolina, at her sister's urging, got up to look at her. But her eyes rested on the newcomer without sympathy. Because of this new little creature, Antonietta had been—for an eternal moment—between the jaws of death. Why had she appeared in this melancholy house?

But contemplating the little rosy clenched fists, she felt pity even for the intruder. If only she was a boy, she thought, she'd have an easier fate. Women are born to serve and suffer. Nothing else.

What was she holding in her little closed fists? Happiness maybe . . . All of us clench our fists at birth so as not to let go of a blessing that we will never find again.

50

Thoughts whirled willy-nilly in her mind. Her head ached, as did her heart. She tiptoed out and went to the kitchen to prepare coffee.

Alessio followed her. In the uncertain light of dawn his frightened little face, with its halo of soft blond hair, looked like a girl's.

Our lives are nothing but habit, as Don Lucio said. For more than two months Antonietta lay in bed, with almost no hope of recovery, and the house went back to its old ways, with only minor alterations here and there, as though its mistress had always been ill. Alessio went to the Dominican school twice a day; Carmelina went to the nuns; Nicolina ran the house, skillful and prompt as always, and also took care of little Agata.

They had finished the noonday meal. The room was warm, full of light, saturated with the heavy odor of food. Carmelina was looking at Alessio, her eyes lively and shining with impatience, so black they looked like the eyes of a mouse. And Alessio was staring at the tablecloth to keep from laughing.

"Can we go?" asked the little, black, mischievous eyes.

"Wait. It's not time yet," replied the gentle brown eyes.

Finally Don Lucio pushed away his plate and made a sign to the children. They could go. Carmelina slid cautiously out of the high chair and ran, followed by her brother, both trying to smother their fresh laughter.

Nicolina cleared the table. She prepared the coffee. She took broth to the sick woman. She knew what had to be done and did it with precision, without losing her patience, walking on tiptoe from the now familiar habit of not disturbing her brother-in-law.

Antonietta, handing back the empty cup, thanked her with her eyes. "Where are the children?" she asked. "What are they doing?"

"They're upstairs. They're playing. Alessio has to go back to school. Carmelina too. He wants her to stay with the nuns until suppertime. He's not going out and it's a nuisance for him to hear her."

"So let her go. She'll be freer at the nuns, poor child. She's so lively!"

And here they were, about to leave. They were still playing and kept shoving each other in the doorway, as they came in to say goodbye to their mother.

"Give us your blessing!"

"Give us your blessing!"

"God bless you, my daughter. God bless you, my son. Don't make so much noise. And be careful of the carriages in the street! Hold each other's hand."

They ran away, laughing. The door could be heard to slam.

"They pay no attention," the mother remarked, smiling.

Nicolina did not answer. For some days she had felt vaguely uneasy at the thought of being left alone with her brother-in-law for the whole afternoon. If only she could keep at least Carmelina with her . . . But she had not dared to go against Don Lucio by expressing her wish. And besides, how could she tell him?

She went back into the dining room to finish a few chores. Then she went to the kitchen and started ironing. It was very warm and she unbuttoned her collar. Thinking she had heard Antonietta call, she went again to the bedroom. She hadn't called and was about to doze off.

"What are you doing, Nicolina?" she asked, opening her eyes.

"I'm ironing. I thought I heard your voice."

"No, Nicolina. I don't need anything. Don't worry."

She drew the blinds and left the darkened room. She went back to her ironing. It was an onerous task at that hour, just after eating, and she looked with a kind of helplessness at the big basket of laundry that stood waiting. It was better—almost better—to be sick, to be able to doze in a cool room . . .

Don Lucio came in slowly, smoking. Nicolina blushed, disturbed and surprised. He never set foot in the kitchen, except in the morning to wash.

"Did you call?" she asked.

"No."

He planted himself in front of the window, his legs spread, and his figure stood out against the background of light like a huge pair of compasses. He was wearing one of his summer suits, with small brown and white checks, which made him look taller.

The buzzing of a fly knocking against the window panes in a vain effort to get out, and the methodical sucking of his lips glued to the stem of the pipe, could be distinctly heard.

"Do you feel warm?"

"A little."

"You should never iron at this hour. You work too hard."

Nicolina blushed more deeply, moved by his unusual remark. Did anyone feel sorry for her? And at this thought she had a violent urge to cry.

53

"I know a lady," said Don Lucio, approaching the table, "who smokes."

"Smokes?" exclaimed Nicolina, trying to be obliging and take an interest in this news.

"Yes. The notary Marullo's sister-in-law. She smokes like a man."

And again the silence became deep, but strained. Don Lucio now seemed engrossed in contemplating the clothes Nicolina was ironing.

"Smoke doesn't bother you?"

"No. I've got used to it."

"That's because you've never had it in your face."

"What an idea!"

"Here, like this." Leaning forward a little, Don Lucio blew a puff of smoke in her face. Nicolina ducked to one side, nauseated. Don Lucio laughed.

"See? You can't stand it."

Nicolina made no reply. The smoke, the fetid air in the kitchen, and most of all the anxiety that once again she felt at the thought of being left alone with him, made her acutely uncomfortable.

So the thing to do was to stop ironing, make some excuse to go to the bedroom, and remain there until the children returned. She must insist that, starting tomorrow, Carmelina stay home and keep her company. But she didn't move; her muscles and nerves went limp and refused to obey her will.

Don Lucio put his arm around her waist, touching her ever so lightly, as when in the dawn he had met her at the foot of the stairs.

Nicolina, setting down the iron, drew away from him and started toward the door, finally making an effort to walk. Don Lucio, without hurrying, caught up with her. He seized her almost violently. Nicolina tried to break free, to flee; she wanted to cry out, but her voice died in her throat. Now Don Lucio was holding her, with only one arm, tightly against his chest. He had stopped laughing. Scowling, as when he gave an order, he said, "Antonietta won't call you."

Still holding her tightly, he crossed the dining room, almost carrying her with his sinewy arm. As they reached the small sitting room, he repeated mechanically:

"Antonietta won't call you."

She had taken refuge in her own room, and now, huddled on the edge of the bed, looking at her pointed knees shaken by a trembling she was unable to check, she was amazed that she had found the strength to climb the stairs. She had lost all awareness of time. Perhaps life slipped away like light. Outside the round window the roofs could be seen turning red in the flaming sunset. And the roofs quivered and slipped away, the bed, the chairs, every object whirled and vanished, a great darkness fell, and then everything came back with a crash and the red light returned.

Antonietta and the children were far away. She thought of Sant'Agata, of her mother. Poor mamma! Why did you let your little girl leave home?

At moments she seemed to be suspended in the void and falling with the light, without being able to catch hold of anything. She heard the voice of the Redhead, the familiar raucous voice in the street outside. It came from far away, that voice. Everything was far away.

What would she do tomorrow? And the day after? She felt disgust, a horror of life. Time passes all the same, indifferent to our miseries and pains. The big clock on the wall goes on murmuring the hours, with no letup. Nothing will change, though hell itself has broken out in the soul.

"God!" she prayed, in anguish. "Let me never see my fellow creatures and the light of day again. Let me die . . ."

Then came a hurried footstep on the stairs, which creaked a little under the light weight. It was Alessio.

"Aunt Nicoli'! Why are you sitting in the dark? Papa says to come and fix supper."

She jumped up. Alessio hugged her, joyfully tugging her along. She pushed him gently away.

"I'm coming," she said. "I'm coming."

"What did I do, Aunt Nicoli'?"

"Nothing. Just leave me alone. I'm coming now."

Her lips would never again dare place themselves on the brows of innocent children. Her kiss had forever lost its purity.

She went downstairs, automatically tying the strings of her dark apron. The room, submerged in the quiet lamplight, seemed filled with peaceful domesticity. Alessio and Carmelina were cutting out pictures from an old book. Don Lucio, busy writing in a ledger, did not raise his eyes on hearing her footsteps.

She went into the kitchen. There she opened the drawer of the table and took out the tablecloth. Is it possible, she thought in anguish, is it possible for everything to be "like before"? And out of habit, she said to Carmelina, "Help me set the table."

But she almost jumped at hearing her own voice, which sounded calm and collected, like before, in the stillness of the room.

II

HAVING finished his homework, Alessio was stacking his books and notebooks on the little table that stood at the foot of Nicolina's bed. He was singing softly.

"*'Io ti seguìa com'iride di pace . . .'*"

All of a sudden he stopped. "Aunt Nicoli', have you ever been to the theater?" he asked, closing the drawer of the table.

"Never."

He went on singing, then stopped again. "You know what, Aunt Nicoli'? A friend of mine has invited me to hear *Manon*. A box seat. It's a real piece of luck . . ."

Nicolina put down her sewing and, sighing, looked out the round garret window. "So you must ask permission."

"It's absolutely no use," Alessio exclaimed.

"Who knows? If you catch him at the right moment."

"It's no use," the boy repeated bitterly. "And even suppose he were to say yes! I would have had to keep asking and asking, and go through all that uncertainty just so I could tell my friend: I'm coming with you. And then you and mamma waiting up for me, and he's waiting and mad. No, no. After all, do you really think you can enjoy something if you have to swallow it whole? Of course not. You need to be in a happy frame of mind, and not have to think about it. And so"—he added after a pause, in a calmer voice—"and so I've told my friend I'm not coming this time either."

"And maybe it's better that way," said Nicolina, relieved.

"It's not better," Alessio replied, once more in heated tones. "At least it's not better for me. I can't live like you, or mamma or Carmelina. You're all women. All it takes is a little sewing in your hands or going to mass on Sunday and you're satisfied. I think about so many things. I want so many things. Sometimes my head spins, I get so carried away. No, it's no use. You'll never understand me!"

"You've got no business complaining, especially about your father, who provides for us all!"

"What's that got to do with it? I'm not complaining. Who's talking about him now? Am I lacking in respect toward him? What's he got to do with it? Is it my fault if I'm not happy? But you don't understand me. You and mamma have got used to it all, like a snail taking the shape of its shell."

"But, Alessio!" cried Nicolina, in a tone of reproach. "You're still a little boy and just because you've learned a few words of Latin you think that gives you the right to judge your elders! Think about growing up first, and don't let your imagination run away with you."

She felt it was her duty to chide him.

"Oh, sure!" said Alessio, forcing himself to smile, since he could feel tears rising to his eyes. "Sure, grow up so that one fine day I can be somebody's administrator, too."

"And that's not an honorable profession?"

"Who says it's not honorable? Just the opposite. *'Di quella pira l'orrendo foco . . .'* "

"And anyway," Nicolina interrupted, "it's not true that you'll be an administrator. How do you know what intentions your father has for you?"

"I just know. I can tell. And that's why it's hopeless. Engineer! 'Alessio Gaspare Carmine, professional engineer.' Sounds great, doesn't it! Or how about 'Carmine Alessio, engineer'? Well, I've got other ambitions. If you only knew how I hate the thought of *having* to take that curriculum . . ."

"Now just calm down. Why do you get so upset? The university is still a long way off! Do you think we have any control over time?"

And Nicolina bowed her head, not daring to reproach her nephew any further.

Boys certainly aren't like girls! They start flapping their wings early! This poor child was like a bird trying to fly inside an iron cage. Who could say what thoughts were going through his little head! But how could anyone keep up with him in his wild daydreams? His eyes, soft and shy as those of a young antelope, already looked farther than women dare to look.

Alessio had gone to get dressed in the little room adjoining his aunt's. He was singing to himself and appeared to be in good spirits again.

There were many things about which he had kept silent. Many things that he did not dare to ask anyone and which had poisoned the wellsprings of his life. No

59

one at home was sincere. How he wished he might say, openheartedly, to Aunt Nicolina:

"Auntie, you mustn't stay here. Go find shelter somewhere, even if it's a convent, but don't go on hurting mamma and yourself by keeping a quarrel going, like a fire we can't put out . . ."

What would Aunt Nicolina's answer have been? In spite of everything, he loved her very much.

Aunt Nicolina, like his mother, had cradled him in her arms; like his mother, she had held him on her knee; she had comforted him, drying his tears with her rough, quick hands, when his father had struck him for some misbehavior.

How many times had Aunt Nicolina, picking him up in her arms and dashing up the stairs, taken refuge in the little room that looked like a ship's cabin, where wordlessly, side by side, their eyes veiled with tears, they had peered together out the round window to watch the roofs turning red and the shifting pattern of gray and pink clouds in the sky! What sad, sweet hours! Their hearts had communed and their thoughts met in a silence filled with bitterness, dejection, and fear.

Yes, he loved this poor aunt of his, frail and thin, whose dark elongated eyes even in anger never lost their expression of dismay. He felt compassion for her. He felt compassion for his mother. A boundless and sorrowing compassion that clouded his young adolescent spirit.

He had been still a child when he understood that "something," very serious and ugly, hung like a shadow over the house that seemed so peaceful. He saw that the two sisters were divided by a sullen and incurable rancor. A word caught on the wing, a bitter quarrel he had witnessed while pretending to be asleep, a glance, a caress he had never forgotten and which had horrified him, had all helped to explain the reason for the discord. And despite it all he had gone on loving his aunt. Sometimes he kept his distance from her. He remained in the same room (she sewing, he pretending to study, with his eyes staring at the same page) without saying a word to her, tormented by a memory, a doubt. But even in those moments he never ceased to feel compassion for her.

" '*Di quella pira* . . .' You know, Aunt Nicoli, today we got a new teacher. He said to me, 'Ah-ha, Alessio Carmine! Aren't you the son of Don Lucio? You used to have an aunt living with you, Nicolina Restivo . . .' 'She's still there,' I said. 'Still there?' he said, surprised. 'She never got married? His name is Professor Casafulli. He's from your village. Did he know you?' "

"Yes, he knew me. What are you laughing about?"

"Oh, nothing. If you could see how funny he looks! He's got a paunch!"

"Who does he live with?"

"With his family, of course! How can you get old and not have a family? He even has a little boy, a little tow-headed boy."

Nicolina frowned. It's true, everyone has a family of his own. But all men are so selfish. To think that her father, God rest his soul . . . Well, no sooner had she gone away than his feelings had changed. Why had he never put in an appearance, never once asked about her?

How could her sister blame her? She had done no harm to anyone. Abandoned by those people who had seemed to her the best, she had grown old in this house

61

like a faithful servant. Whom had she harmed but herself? Whom had she deceived but herself? She was like someone biting into a spoiled fruit that leaves a bitter taste in the mouth.

Alessio picked up his books. "I'm going. *Salve*, Aunt Nicolina, *puella sedula.* . ."

"I'm going downstairs too. Why do you say *salve*?"

"It's Latin for goodbye. They also say *ave.*"

"Don't make jokes with the words of the saints! It's a sin!" Nicolina admonished. "And you're too disrespectful."

They went down the stairs together, almost racing.

"Look what you make me do!" Nicolina kept repeating, laughing and letting herself be dragged along. "You'd think I was your age!"

Antonietta was in the back room with the little girls.

"Give me your blessing, mamma!" cried Alessio, while Nicolina went out on the terrace to hang some laundry. "I'm off to school."

"God bless you, my son. Aren't you taking an umbrella?"

"But look how sunny it is!"

"I can see clouds over there. And the school is so far away."

"What d'you mean, far away!"

The boy lingered. Whenever he went out, he had a great desire to leave his mother with a kind word, but he didn't know what to say. How he wished they could all live in peace and harmony!

"Go out on the terrace!" he cried. "Let Agatina get a little air—she never goes out! It's such a beautiful day!"

He left, slamming the door behind him, if only to

make some noise and shake up the too silent house. He went down the stairs four at a time, singing at the top of his lungs. And then he felt as though he were cata-pulting out of the narrow street and into the broad one full of sunlight and movement.

"Here's papa!" Agata announced.

Antonietta got up and went to help in the kitchen.

When Don Lucio was home, the two women made an effort not to display too openly the hatred that di-vided them and in which they were obliged to live together, like two pairs of scissors in the same sheath.

Antonietta, recovering, had made violent scenes. But Don Lucio had been able to cut short any grounds for recrimination with two irrefutable arguments: first, that it was all Antonietta's fault for having so often neglected her duties by not sufficiently supervising her younger sister (whose mincing ways would have turned the head of a hermit!) and paying more attention to her children than to her husband; second, that he, Don Lucio, with his heart condition, from which he might die any minute, needed absolute peace and quiet. The wrangling of the two sisters, and his wife's tantrums, would turn his existence into a living hell! Further-more, the problems of the little family in Sant'Agata, their constant need to ask for one thing or another, had helped to silence Antonietta in her husband's presence. Antonio was coming to the city for a competition, Al-fonso to take the exams for his high-school diploma, the land had been mortgaged . . . And Don Lucio was on hand, ready to give hospitality to his brothers-in-law, important advice to his mother-in-law, even to lend not insignificant sums, without a guarantee.

Didn't he at least deserve to be rewarded with a little peace in the family?

Carmelina had laid the table, slowly in order to gain time, and Nicolina had twice come to the doorway to check on her brother-in-law's place setting. Nothing was missing: there was his saltcellar, his toothpick holder, the plate of salami on one side, the rye rolls on the other.

"Are you ready?"

"Everything's ready. We'll serve in a moment."

Alessio was getting to be a pain in the neck! "Shall I wait a little longer?" Nicolina suggested.

"Yes, you'd better," replied Antonietta, without looking at her.

Carmelina went to peer out through the grating that gave on the stairway. She came back downcast. "He's not coming!"

They heard the voice of Don Lucio, who for the past several minutes had been impatiently clinking his knife against his plate. "So do we eat or not? What are we waiting for? What's going on here?"

They brought the food to the table at once. While Antonietta broke pieces of bread for the little girls, Don Lucio, motioning to the empty chair with his head, asked, "Where did he go?"

"To school."

"To school!" Don Lucio repeated ironically, raising his eyes to the ornate clock on the wall.

They gulped down their soup without tasting it. While Don Lucio went on munching slowly, his eyes half-closed, the two sisters rushed back to the kitchen with the excuse of seeing to the roast. Carmelina fidgeted in her chair, eager to get up and see if her brother was coming, pricking up her ears at every noise on the stairs. There he is now . . . No, it's the widow's door opening, it's a heavy step on the landing, it's someone knocking on the second floor.

"Stop that! Can't you learn to sit still?" Don Lucio admonished, touching the riding crop that he kept hanging on the back of the chair. Carmelina cringed, as though she had been struck.

Someone's ringing. He's finally back!

Yes, it's Alessio, flushed and overheated; he's been on the beach with his friends. For his sisters he has a pocketful of little colored pebbles that look like sugar-coated almonds, and he shows some to Agata. He is still perspiring, excited; the sun itself seems to glow in his eyes.

"Be quiet, Alessio. Calm down. Papa is angry," whispered his aunt.

His father's voice asking harshly, "Where have you been?", the silence of what feels like a cold dining room, the distressed faces of the women, all this suddenly depressed him.

He sat down, dejected, and began eating greedily. He was jolted by the voice of his father, who, holding a piece of light, tasty-smelling roast impaled on his fork, was again asking:

"Where ex-act-ly have you been?"

"We came back the long way, on the Palazzata side."

"Don't you know you're supposed to be here at five o'clock sharp?"

The little girls had been finished for some time. They were impatient to get up from the table, to see the pebbles that Alessio had in his pocket along with a few strands of rank seaweed and some still wet limpets.

They kept peering at their father, waiting for him to give the signal, glad that he had not scolded Alessio as severely as they had expected. Agata was the first to slide cautiously from the high chair, and at the door she called the others by waving her hands. Carmelina took heart and asked, "Can we go now, papa?"

"Go. Remember that when I call you at eight o'clock, your homework has to be done."

The little girls sighed. Away they went, up the wooden stairs, which, as Alessio liked to say, creaked loudly with pleasure from being loved by the children, and into the garret rooms, the outlet and refuge for their first small sorrows, their noisy games, and open laughter.

"Run, Agatina. It's our castle! Alessio? What's the matter?"

Slowly and joylessly, Alessio followed them.

Antonietta, having emptied the small mattresses, was getting ready to beat the stuffing. Nicolina came in to help her, as though she had been summoned. Without speaking, she knotted a kerchief around her head and began beating with one of the rods. They appeared to have reached sufficient agreement beforehand as to each one's task. Having finished beating, they stood up at the same time, shook off the dust and threads that had clung to their black aprons, and began to refill the red and white cover that lay limply in a corner like a soiled rag. They were hurrying to finish before Don Lucio, who insisted on finding the house in order and his women tidy, returned home. Having spread the cover across two boards, Antonietta began refilling it with the wool that Nicolina brought her by the armful. Already she was tired. A little plump and heavy, she panted with the effort. Nicolina went back and forth with the wool in her arms without getting out of breath. Almost without thinking, she still reserved for herself the more tiring chores and spared her sister, in accordance with the habit of so many years. She swept up the fluff left on the floor and emptied a second mattress. Then she threaded a needle and, still silent as by a tacit understanding, began to sew the long slit from the end opposite to the one her sister had begun working on.

"Get the stool," said Antonietta, raising her eyes and seeing her sister bending over uncomfortably. "It's on the balcony. As you can see, I'm sitting down."

The youngest child had left some of her toys on the stool. "Agatina," said Nicolina as she approached the balcony, "please take these things off and let me have the stool."

"It's mine," the child replied. "And I won't give it to you."

"That's rude!"cried Alessio, who had just come in. "You don't have to give it to her as a present! If there aren't any more chairs—"

"What do I care?" replied the child, leaning on the stool with both hands to defend it. Then she shrieked, "She can't order me around! This is mamma's house! It's not her house!"

Nicolina staggered. Antonietta went pale and stood up, and seizing the child by the arm, dragged her into the next room.

"Mamma said so! Mamma said so!" screamed Agatina, struggling to free herself.

"Alessio," Antonietta ordered, "take her upstairs with you."

She came back and sat down. But her hands were visibly trembling as she resumed her interrupted sewing. Nicolina was still standing near the balcony, where they had left her, her arms dangling at her sides.

"There," she said as she came back, "you see what you've accomplished by letting your children hear your outbursts. They repeat *your* words. I'm an outsider, an enemy, in *your* house. Especially to the girls, the little one in particular. She's grown up in the middle of our quarrels, as though in a cradle of nettles."

She fell silent and hid her face in her hands. Antonietta went on sewing. In the deep silence that filled the room, bitter words passed back and forth unspoken. The two women's hearts beat violently, like those of two children waiting for the thunder to roar after the lightning.

"It's the truth," Antonietta said finally. "Is it my fault perhaps? Your presence is a scandal to my children."

"Shut up! Shut up! Alessio might hear. He, at least, has loved me since he was a little boy!"

"He's upstairs. With Agata. I heard him go up. And besides, you think he doesn't understand? Children keep their eyes wide open nowadays . . ."

"Shut up," Nicolina repeated, straining to listen. No, Alessio couldn't hear them . . .

But the boy had left his little sister busily cutting out pictures from the newspaper, and had tiptoed back. He was listening, with a lump of grief in his throat.

"He's not there," Antonietta repeated. She too had risen. Aroused by their exertion, they stared at each other in defiance. It seldom happened that they found themselves completely alone, face to face, but when it did it took only a trifle, an incautious word or gesture, to cause a flaring of the too long muted hatred that smoldered in their breasts. They spoke in muffled voices, instinctively clenching their fists.

Two bright red spots, like two brushstrokes, tinged the sharp cheekbones on Nicolina's sallow face. "Yes, it's your fault," she charged. "Yours. No one else's. You've ruined my life. And now you'd like to kick me out? Well, I'm not going. I've told you. I won't leave this house alive. I've wasted my carefree youth here, like a veil dropped on a thornbush. You've ruined me. You threw me to the wolf. Your selfishness made you lazy, and so you left it up to me to wait on him, for days on end. Did it suit you then for me to play servant to you and your children? Did it suit you? And didn't it ever occur to you that I was a poor creature made of flesh, like you? Why should you have been the only one to love him? Wasn't I capable of feeling *then*—not now! not any more! not any more!—what you felt? And even more deeply than you? You didn't think of that? And if you did think of it, doesn't that make you more depraved than the most depraved of women?"

"I trusted you," murmured Antonietta. "You were my little sister. You were Nicolinedda . . . I never thought. I never thought," she repeated with a doleful cry, pressing her hands to her forehead. "How could I imagine that my own flesh and blood would betray me? I had no idea I was housing a serpent in my bosom. I should have kept an eye on you. I would have seen from your face that you weren't a good person. Look at yourself! Look at yourself in the mirror, you hussy! You have the face of sin! The bony, haggard face of someone who betrays her own flesh and blood . . ."

69

"It's your fault!"

"Mine! If only you'd gone away immediately, *then—*"

"*Your* fault!"

"—when the children were still little . . ."

"No. I couldn't go away. I couldn't leave this God-forsaken house. I would have gone away like a body without a soul. Go away! Like an old dishrag that's no good for anything any more! Like a squeezed lemon thrown in the middle of the street! My mother had entrusted me to you. It would have meant going back in humiliation, when I would have been unable to pretend, old already without having lived whatever life I had coming to me. Her poor eyes, worn out with crying, would have looked at me and cried more bitterly than ever. And my brothers? How would they have greeted me? And Caterina? Caterina knows nothing about sin and has no sympathy for those who fall."

"Go now. Go! It's not too late. They won't know anything about it unless you tell them. It's up to you. Leave me in peace, at least now!" Antonietta repeated, in anguish. "Have pity, not for me but for my children. In your place, I would have run away, vanished, a thousand times. You love the girls and yet you don't scruple to be a scandal to their innocent souls."

"They wouldn't understand, you miserable woman, if you didn't let them hear you. You've even gone so far as to say bad things about me to Carmelina! No!" she repeated, "I'm not leaving. You want to be left quietly in *your* house, among *your* children! No! You'll drag the chain with me. I've been living on the crumbs of your charity like Lazarus at the rich man's table. You're throwing me out so as to be left in peace? And what

right do you have to your peace? Isn't it more than
enough that I—I who adored him *then* without knowing it—I who waited on him with more devotion than
you—"

She broke off, looking around in dismay. The key
was heard turning in the lock. It must have been half
past four.

Alessio slunk away. The two sisters, their hands
chilled and trembling, tried to resume their work. Once
again the house was immersed in a silence that was
like the water of a lake gradually finding its level.

Don Lucio, tall and dressed in green, appeared in the
doorway.

"Are you still there?" he grumbled, annoyed.

Antonietta went to the kitchen. Nicolina brought
her brother-in-law's slippers and placed them in front
of the armchair; then she too decided to go into the
kitchen.

Alessio had taken refuge in the darkness of his little
room. His head in his hands, he wept his grief. His
heart overflowed with pity for his mother, pity for his
aunt. Twice he had tried to screw up his courage to go
down and with a few soothing words make peace between the two sisters. But he hadn't dared. His presence would only have brought new and greater pain for
both of them.

There was no way he could intercede. He was still a
boy, a poor boy who was not supposed to understand,
not supposed to "judge his elders." He felt deeply hurt
and humiliated; it was as though the world had suddenly dimmed, and every hope, every thing of beauty,
had been swallowed up in a boundless sadness.

He could never forget the occasional quarrels he had

71

witnessed unseen. Even in his brightest hours, a thin and tenacious vein of melancholy always ran through his adolescent spirit. Yes, there was *something* that made life ugly!—like a spot impossible to rub out.

"Alessio! Come to the table!"

He jumped up in confusion. He washed his face to remove the traces of his tears.

He sat down and ate in silence, with no appetite. His eyes were red, and his finespun hair, still damp, clung to his translucent temples. But Don Lucio, intent on chewing slowly as an aid to digestion, paid no attention to his son. Nor did the two sisters, still somewhat upset, pay him any mind.

They were making sausages at home, under the expert guidance of Don Lucio.

He had a small meat grinder, and kept a piece of cork stuck with twenty or more pins with which to prick each portion evenly. When sausage-making time came, every December, there was no need to go searching for unsuitable pins or hatpins, which make holes and ruin everything, as happens in so many families.

With his own hands, he had measured and weighed the salt, pepper, and fennel seed; and now that the filling was ready and the women were stuffing the casings, he was intent on properly applying his piece of cork. Even the little girls, delighted by the novelty of it, enjoyed helping. It was as though the holiday had already come. This is how it always is when Christmas is approaching and the sideboard overflows with good things to eat.

Only Alessio was missing. It was his last day of school and he was late, as usual.

If only Aunt Nicolina could see him! He was dawdling, almost without realizing it, for the sheer pleasure of dawdling. He enjoyed letting himself be carried
along by the moving crowd in the street, like a straw
abandoned to the current of a river. At one point he
stopped to look at a quantity of toys that could hardly
have interested him; at another he was fascinated to
watch two men pasting up a poster as big as a sheet;
farther on he wormed his way into the middle of a
cluster of people to find out what was going on. Finally
he stood for a while engrossed in contemplating a display of old books. He would have liked to buy *The
Lives of Famous Men*, but did not have the seventy-five
centesimi asked by the bookseller.

"Some other time . . ." he said, a little embarrassed,
as he walked away.

Approaching home, he quickened his pace. At the
corner a woman dressed in black stepped out in front of
him. Her face was gaunt and wrinkled, and glowered
like the face of a gypsy. He tried to slip past her. But the
woman stopped him.

"Don't be afraid of a poor unfortunate woman.
Aren't you the son of Don Lucio Carmine?"

"Yes."

"Baron Rossi's right-hand man?"

"His agent, you mean?"

"It's the same thing. Look. He, your papa, won't listen
to me. I've pleaded with him like you plead with a saint
on the altar, and he told me to get out. Wait and hear
what I have to say, for the love you must have for your
mother. Three months ago I pawned my poor daughter's
necklace with him, in the ground-floor room of the Casa
de' Venti, where he does his business. It's a beautiful

73

necklace and rather old. He wanted some sort of guarantee. He promised he'd let me redeem the jewel as soon as he had his money back, with no time limit. I brought him the money—it wasn't even all that much!—and he told me that his obligation was only for two months and he doesn't have the necklace any more! Oh, what a shock, signorino! You tell him. You have the face of a little Saint Anthony, and your heart can't be bad . . ."

"But I don't understand. Papa couldn't have lent you money!"

"Would that he never had! Would that I'd gone to a pawnbroker! At least I wouldn't have got caught in a swindle."

"I don't believe you."

"May the Madonna strike me blind if I'm lying. May I not live to see the holy day of Christmas if I'm not telling you the truth."

"It can't be," exclaimed Alessio, and again tried to go past her. But the woman seized his hand and kept talking to him, her burning eyes fixed on him with an expression of supplication, suffering, and hatred.

"I'll tell papa," Alessio said finally, a little frightened by the unknown woman's gypsy look. "I don't believe that he lent you money. I absolutely don't believe it. But I'll speak to him about it anyway. Yes, even if I get a beating for it, I'll tell him what you've told me. If it's true," he murmured through his tears, "you'll get your necklace back. But what should I say so he'll know who you are?"

"Oh, he knows! Tell him Maria from Three Kings' Lane. You can't mistake the necklace. It's old. In the middle there's a little gold cross set with red stones, so red they look like drops of blood. He knows. You can bet your life he knows!"

Alessio rushed up the stairs. He was given a scolding.

"Where ex-act-ly have you been?"

He paid no attention to the scolding. Later he couldn't remember what excuses he had offered. He felt dazed. The woman's words kept churning in his mind. How can I tell him? he thought, how can I tell him? And meeting his father's sleepy, tranquil gaze, he winced and lowered his eyes. It can't be true! he repeated to himself. It can't be. I won't have the courage to open my mouth.

All evening he struggled manfully with himself. He went to bed without having spoken.

"Goodnight. Give me your blessing . . . Give me your blessing . . ."

Next morning he sighed with relief when his father left the house on business. Then he was impatient for his return. Again it was evening and he hadn't opened his mouth. Nicolina lighted the lamp. Antonietta brought the briefcase with the ledgers to the table. The house was peaceful and quiet.

I'm the only one, the only one who's burning up inside, thought Alessio.

He simply had to speak, to get rid of this scorching pain. Maybe it would be better to ask his mother's advice. He'll never forgive me, he thought, for believing the accusations of a woman in the street. But then all he had to do was to tell what had happened, showing that he hadn't believed her.

"Papa!" he exclaimed with determination. But his voice cracked.

"Wait a minute," said Don Lucio, putting down his pipe and getting up.

"He's going to get my present!" whispered Carmelina, blushing with joy. "He promised it to me yesterday."

Don Lucio returned with a small packet. Very slowly he unwrapped it, keeping the women's curiosity in suspense.

"How beautiful!" cried Antonietta.

"How beautiful!" repeated Nicolina.

Alessio stood up to look, and went white as wax.

"No! No!" he cried, shaken by a convulsive tremor. "Don't give it to her, papa! I beg you!"

Dangling in his hands, Don Lucio was holding a fine necklace of antique gold, a little gold cross with red stones.

"What's the matter with you?" said Nicolina, making him sit down. But Alessio struggled to his feet again.

"No. Don't give it to her!"

He was trembling all over, pushed to the limit by the bottled-up emotions of twenty-four hours.

"So?" exclaimed Don Lucio, banging a threatening fist on the table. "Do you mind telling me what's the matter?"

"Don't frighten him," Antonietta pleaded. "He must be sick. Don't you see how upset he is?"

"If he's sick, he should be treated. If he's crazy, he should be put in a lunatic asylum."

"I'm not sick! I'm not crazy!" exclaimed Alessio. And in a halting voice he recounted the scene of the day before, without omitting a word, since every word had remained stamped on his memory.

Don Lucio listened without interrupting, without moving a muscle of his face. Better to let him say it all, and not make him suspicious. But this boy, who went snooping around and found out about everything, was a dangerous little judge. Making an effort to control himself, he caressed his son and explained to him and the women that he had bought the necklace from an antique jeweler, and had paid a handsome price for it.

"Maria from Three Kings' Lane—"

"Yes, Maria from the lane. I know her. She used to work as a servant in the notary's house. That's how I know her. She saw me buying it. She's trying a little blackmail. She's a good-for-nothing woman, a thief. She's already had a run-in with the police. The city is full of such people. She accosted you because you're a child and don't understand anything. I know because I have to look after thirty or more ground-floor flats rented to crooked types like Maria from Three Kings' Lane. They come one after another! I've warned you again and again: don't stop and talk to people we don't know!"

He spoke through clenched teeth to control his anger. Alessio felt stricken: his ears were buzzing, and finally he lost consciousness. They carried him to bed, like a child. He had an attack of fever.

"Nervous fever," Don Lucio declared, when next morning he went upstairs to see him. "He'll learn what life is all about."

For two days, as long as the delirium lasted, he did not leave the sick boy's bedside, fearful lest he let slip something previously left unsaid.

And Don Lucio was relieved: Alessio knew nothing except that stupid business of the necklace. But he was unable to overcome the vague feeling of distrust that his son, the only one in the house who eluded his vigilant surveillance, inspired in him.

The jewel disappeared into the ebony box, and Carmelina wept for her lost present. The briefcase also disappeared from the shelf near the balcony; in the evening Don Lucio got up to retrieve it himself from a locked drawer.

Alessio, after the unhappy Christmas holidays, returned to school, weakened by fever, and he did not encounter any more troublemakers. He felt humiliated at having been taken in, and yet a small insistent doubt continued for some time to torment him. He was afraid, especially toward dusk, of running into the woman dressed in black, with her gypsy face: she must be lurking there by the wall, waiting for him, her dark burning eyes filled with hatred and supplication.

But his father had not lied. He kept seeing him as he had seen him that evening, calm, persuasive, mildly offended, mildly indulgent. He hadn't lied.

Still what had happened to the necklace? Why had it not been given to Carmelina, if it had been purchased? The mere thought of the little cross of antique gold, set with red stones, so red they looked like drops of blood, struck him with horror.

Don Lucio was leaving on his annual business trip, to inspect and settle the baron's holdings; afterwards he planned to go to Catania and pay a visit to his married sisters, who would send him away loaded with food and gifts. Ever since he had realized that his sisters would not be a nuisance to him, he thought of them each year with a certain fondness.

78

"Ah, yes indeed!" he would say, convinced of being sincerely moved. "Blood is thicker than water!"

And so saying, he would endeavor to pack into his suitcases and hampers all the preserves, fruit, and sponge cake that the sisters were sending to their little nieces, whom they had never met. In those moments, they even forgot how their only brother had abandoned them at the time when they had been left orphans and without a future.

Everything was ready for his departure. The little girls, who had not been sent to the nuns that day so that they could say goodbye to their father, were shouting and chasing each other in the small courtyard where Alessio had carried the suitcases, two large black leather suitcases with covers of jute cloth and sporting the initials "L.M.C." adorned with red and yellow sprigs.

The women, weeping as they did every year, tried to detain Don Lucio a while at the door, giving him greetings to take to the family in Sant'Agata. Nicolina, seizing her brother-in-law's hand, covered it with kisses as she repeated a beloved name, a name that pained her heart every time she uttered it aloud.

"Mamma . . . Tell mamma that . . ."

Antonietta did not mind her sister saying goodbye to the traveler with the same passionate tenderness with which she herself had said goodbye to him. It was a fleeting moment of deep sincerity, in which each woman read the other's heart.

They were not weeping for him—oh no! They were thinking fervently of the places he would be seeing again and which they had not set eyes on for so many years. And through their nostalgia for the past, which

79

flooded their hearts, ran a thread of fear for the days to come. It was the fear of remaining by themselves, face to face, like two culprits locked in the same cell—with no escape.

With Don Lucio absent and the children at school, there was never any reason for silence. Quarrels broke out more violently, more frequently. A few days would go by in peace and quiet if Nicolina stayed shut up in her little room in the "pigeon loft," and Antonietta in the back room of the house. They would see each other only at mealtimes, and even then they would often not see each other, since with the master of the house away, they did not bother to cook every day but would grab a bite in passing, between one household chore and another. Days of painful quiet, of unnerving silences, or hellish days—these were what awaited them.

The impatient cracking of the driver's whip could be heard outside.

"Let me go," said Don Lucio, and started down the stairs, followed by the women. They knew that when he reached the next to last landing, he would turn around, and at a certain point they stopped. Don Lucio stopped at the next to last landing and turned, frowning under his checkered cap.

"What is today?"

"Saturday," Antonietta replied.

"It's the fifteenth," Nicolina added.

Don Lucio consulted his pocket notebook, where he had marked the whole itinerary of his trip, and announced: "I'll be back the thirtieth of next month by the six-twenty train." And he continued down the stairs.

He, who divided his time with mathematical precision, did not believe in the unforeseen events that strike so many men. If he said the thirtieth, he would be back on the thirtieth, by the six-twenty train, reaching home by carriage at seven. He expected to find the broth and the roast ready, fresh linen folded at the foot of the bed, and hot water to wash.

He kissed the little girls and, after repeatedly admonishing him in a humdrum voice, he kissed Alessio. He embraced his wife, and then, without hesitation, solemnly squeezed his sister-in-law's hand and gave her a fraternal kiss on the forehead. Whereupon Nicolina burst into fresh tears and her example was followed, like an echo, by Antonietta and the girls. Now they were truly alone.

"Goodbye! Goodbye!"

"Give us your blessing, papa!"

The stairs resounded with sobs. For, after all, he was the only person who really loved them.

Was it his fault? Antonietta wondered, as she went back up the stairs. Was it his fault if fate had ordained that *she* should become attached to his life like a flimsy thread entangled in the branches of a tree? And hadn't *she* perhaps atoned? Their hearts were brimming with the same feeling of sympathy. One in front, the other behind on the stairs, they had the same impulse: to speak kindly to each other without further ado, since they had both been deceived by life and ought to forgive each other . . .

But as soon as the door, which creaked dully on its hinges, was closed again, they were struck by the same old chill, and their incurable rancor sustained them anew.

Agata was jumping up and down in the vestibule,

pushing her sister, happy that their father had left and that for a while they could romp freely, without the threat of the terrible riding crop.

Nicolina was seized with anger, almost as though this burst of joy had been provoked by her unjustifiable tears. "You heartless girl!" she cried, giving Agata a good shaking. "Papa isn't even at the station and you're already laughing!"

She ran to take refuge in her room so as to weep her tears alone, tears to which she had no right at that moment without being judged and mocked. Agata, the youngest, the one who had imbibed enmity against her with her mother's milk, was mocking her. Yes, mocking her . . .

"Well?" Alessio repeated insistently.

"I don't know . . . Papa's not here . . . It would look like we were taking advantage of his absence . . ."

"To take a simple little walk?" asked Alessio. "Come on, mamma, don't exaggerate! Make up your mind, at least for Carmelina and Agata, who never see a ray of sunshine! When papa's here, there's not enough time. When he's not here . . ."

Antonietta did not reply. It was a tempting idea to lock the door behind her and go out on a carefree excursion with her children. But she saw an obstacle in coming to an agreement with her sister, who would criticize her and might even accuse her of frivolity when Don Lucio returned.

"Well," she said finally, and it was as though a veil had darkened her pale flaccid face. "Take your aunt. I wouldn't like your father to come back and find the door locked."

"Papa's not coming back today," cried Alessio, and ran to call his aunt.

Nicolina let herself be pulled, smiling, into the bedroom. "Alessio, let go of me! Where are you taking me?"

She was glad that her nephew was forcing her to enter her sister's room. Antonietta, too, hearing the playful squabble, was happy that her son was placing himself between them, like an angel of peace. Yet Nicolina, as she set foot on the threshold, regretted having come in, while Antonietta stiffened unintentionally.

"Alessio dragged me here," Nicolina explained, embarrassed. "He says we ought to go out."

"If you think he'd like it," said Antonietta, without raising her eyes. "It's a nice day and the girls have no school . . ."

"What should I wear?" asked Nicolina after a few minutes of silence. "My summer dress?"

"Yes!" Alessio replied cheerfully. "Everybody's wearing summer clothes now."

It took the two sisters a long time to get dressed, since they were unaccustomed to going out and could not immediately find all the necessary little accessories. There was a moment of confusion.

"Agata, let me have the shoehorn!"

"Ask mamma where are my gloves!"

"Carmelina, run and get your skirt, it must be in your aunt's closet."

And then there were belts that no longer fastened, buttons that popped seemingly out of spite, and wrinkled sleeves that needed to be ironed.

"Summer dresses and winter hats!" Nicolina murmured unhappily, looking at herself in the mirror.

They kept searching for things they had forgotten, lamenting that they had wasted too much time, that they had decided too late to go out. But finally they were ready. Finally they got free of the house.

By a tacit agreement Antonietta stayed behind with the girls. Nicolina walked in front with her nephew, who was filled with pride at having taken the family out like a grown man, and every few steps turned around to smile at his mother with an air of saying to her: "I'm walking with my aunt so that she won't be alone, but I'd just as soon walk with you!" In his heart there was always the sorrowful, perpetual wish to see his mother and aunt living in harmony.

He thought: When I grow up and have a wife and children, I'll take them out for a walk every day and I'll spend all the money I earn to make them happy!

A few people turned around to stare at the little band. Two young men smiled and one of them said, "They look like something out of one of my great-grandmother's fashion plates."

Indeed, the two women, by no means old, in their ungainly dresses with ruffles and flounces, their velvet hooded capes, looked quite incongruous in the colorful and animated setting of the street. For—unfortunately—it was the promenade hour.

Alessio was ashamed. He tried unsuccessfully to steer them away from the overcrowded fashionable streets, and had nothing more to say. He sensed that "his women" were badly dressed, and when he passed alongside an elegant lady, he lowered his eyes and blushed.

Why? he asked himself bitterly. Why must we almost be outcasts? Why does our life have to be so poor and gray, as though in shadow, while the world is beautiful and full of light, and all *other* people are happy?

And he walked on, embarrassed and dismayed, his head drooping, sorry to have taken the family out. The Palazzata looked larger and more splendid to him, the street vaster and more crowded than usual, and it seemed to him that the Neptune at the top was looking down at him with sympathy.

When they reached the open beach, at an almost deserted spot, he felt more cheerful. The boundless and mysterious sea always soothed his spirit. Farther along, where people were still promenading, the sea looked different.

"I'm going to be a sailor," he announced, ending a rapid train of thought.

"God forbid!" exclaimed Nicolina, sitting down on a stone. "Such a dangerous life!"

"I'd be worried sick," Antonietta added, "thinking of you out in the middle of the sea."

"Never mind!" said Alessio. He wanted to say, "Never mind, I'm going to *have* to be an engineer!"

And once again his heart was gripped by a feeling of discontent. But immediately the pleasure he derived from looking at the sea shone in his large girlish eyes.

All three were silent, immersed in a calm filled with tender emotions. The little girls were playing in the sand, collecting pebbles and shells, and uttering little cries of joy at discovering all the curious things that the sea, with a vast rumble, throws up and takes back.

85

"Look," said Alessio. "There's a brigantine out there."

And the eyes of the two sisters sought out the bright and distant speck that Alessio had called a brigantine. Thought seemed suspended in the luminous air, like golden dust. All the little miseries that seemed so huge, the harsh rancor that saturated the air in the house on the narrow street and which they carried locked in their hearts, seemed to disperse and disappear in the serene remoteness of the open sky. Everything was small and far away, like the brigantine sailing by on the sea.

Dusk caught them in the same place, motionless and unmindful. They saw the fiery sun sink into the sea, amid a brilliant purple light that slowly faded. The little girls, excited by the air and freedom, were still chasing each other with shrieks on the beach. The hour was filled with a gentle melancholy.

"I'm going to be a poet . . ." said Alessio.

Nicolina laughed. "You change professions a hundred times a day. Thank goodness there's someone to guide you!"

Alessio frowned, hurt by the tone of that too familiar voice, which brought him back to the reality of things just when he thought he had left them behind.

They walked home abreast, since now the streets were not crowded.

"What a nice walk you made us take!" said Antonietta.

"We ought to do it again, even when Lucio comes back. We'll all be the better for it. Tonight I feel as calm and contented as though I'd taken a hot bath."

They all laughed cheerfully, even the little girls, at Nicolina's comparison.

Nearing home, the two women felt a kind of apprehension. They quickened their pace, almost as though they expected to find Don Lucio waiting, irritated and impatient. They ran up the stairs. They changed their clothes in a hurry, almost as though Don Lucio were there to scold them for having gone out without preparing his pipe and lemonade.

It was the gray and methodical habit of so many years—from which they would never be freed.

He ran to the beach, where he cautiously climbed out along the familiar rocks. He liked to go as far as he could and feel the spray from the surf on his face and hands. He sat crouched there for a while, motionless, his chin in his hands, watching the white waves that came, one after another, to break impetuously on the brown shore.

Something was bothering him and he didn't know what it was. Maybe nothing. Maybe everything. He was living one of his hours of desolation, in which his spirit winced at the slightest fleeting sensation, like a violin string that vibrates and moans when plucked by a finger. Near the school a street musician had been playing a barrel organ; he had run away so as not to hear it, overcome by a sudden wish to cry.

Gradually he was soothed by the sight of the peaceful, boundless sea.

Yes, there was something that made life ugly. He was gripped by feelings of pain and shame. Fleeting images passed repeatedly before his eyes, which were clouded with tears. Here was Aunt Nicolina, clinging to the house the way lichen clings to the rock and doesn't let it breathe. Here was Maria from Three

87

Kings' Lane, pursuing him with her dark angry gaze. Oh, if only he could be relieved of this turmoil that feeds on nothing and mars the spirit, like rust corroding new metal!

Maybe he was mistaken. Maybe his judgment was wrong because he was inexperienced. He did not know how to tell what was good from what was bad and found the most natural actions culpable, the way a child, shut up in a dark room, is afraid of familiar objects.

How he sometimes envied his best friend, whose father indulgently welcomed every little expression of intimacy, and took an interest in the books, friends, escapades, and all things good and bad that made up his son's existence! How many times he had felt an irresistible need to speak to him!

"Baron Rossi, sir!" The first words came readily to his tongue. "I'm just a poor boy who doesn't understand anything . . ."

A boy who suffers and is afraid, because he feels the first instincts of adolescence coiling in his blood like some new illness. A boy still, who needs his mother's kiss at night, and even more needs for his father to guide him step by step toward manhood.

"Baron Rossi, sir . . ."

His thoughts ran to his aunt, to the necklace. What if the things he might say should harm someone? Better to keep silent, since he did not know how to distinguish what was good from what was bad. But was he really suffering because of the family quarrels, and the suspicion that his father had lent money like a usurer? No, no. His discontent lay within himself, like a bitter taste.

Somewhere he had read: "We carry heaven and hell in our hearts." It was unjust that someone who had never harmed anyone should carry hell in his heart.

Now that he attended the gymnasium he no longer went to confession: he would have been ashamed to appear in church. Now he was studying the "evolution of the species," and learning that man descends from the apes and that the sky is nothing but air. But these truths, too, authoritatively delivered from the lecture platform by Professor Friland, perturbed his mind. A few years earlier, Professor Zermani had explained the same things differently, in the same assured tones that allowed for no doubts. So, wondered Alessio, which one knows the truth?

Professor Friland, of course, he answered himself, because he's talking to older boys. Of course . . . But Professor Zermani too had been an intelligent and reasonable man. Had he spent his boyhood on books just to learn a lot of errors? Only errors?

But then why should there have to be errors? He raised his eyes. Not a single cloud was passing in the shining sky. And was there nothing at all beyond that splendid blue serenity?

He gazed at the sea and thought with a shiver of its boundless depths. "No," he repeated aloud, "it can't be that there's nothing beyond the sky!"

"Are you speaking to me, signorino?"

A skinny little old man, in shirtsleeves, was standing in the water up to his knees.

"No, no . . ." exclaimed Alessio, blushing, while all his daydreaming thoughts fled like a swarm of bees in the sun. "What are you looking for?"

The old man thrust a hand in the pocket of his trousers and pulled out a sea urchin and a handful of limpets. Without speaking, he offered them to Alessio.

"Would you like me to open them?"

"Thank you! But I have nothing with me . . . All I have is ten centesimi. Take them."

The old man took the coin, smiling, and with a pocket knife opened the sea urchin. Still smiling, he opened another, offering the bright red innards in their black shell with a calm slow gesture.

"Will you be here tomorrow? I come every day, after school."

"Yes, I'll be here," replied the old man, resuming his search among the rocks.

"Are you a fisherman?"

"No, I'm a peasant. But I can't work because there's been too much rain. So I come here. The sea is good for your health and always has something to give you." And he added: "My son is in America. He didn't want to stay with me any more."

"So you're all alone with your wife?"

"I'm alone. My wife passed away. I had ten children, both boys and girls. Now some are dead, some are married, some are in America, and I'm left behind like a branch with no leaves. God's will be done!"

And the old man smiled kindly, with resignation, spreading his arms. Perhaps he was smiling at his loved ones who had died.

"Goodbye, old fellow," said Alessio, jumping to his feet.

"I kiss your hands, signorino. Do you mind if I tell you something? Just a moment ago you were sitting there looking like a sparrow whose wings had been clipped. Look, when you're young you ought to be happy."

"And if it's no use being young?"

"How can you say such a thing when your hair isn't white? It's always good to be young. I kiss your hands, signorino."

It must be late. Alessio was lectured when he got home. But he paid no attention to the unpleasant welcome he received. In his ears was the lilting voice of the old peasant, and in his heart a quiet will to be good.

For all the misfortunes that had passed over the old man's head, his smile had not lost its childlike sweetness nor his eyes the resigned expression of faith. He seemed to know the deep and humble truths of life.

I'll go back and see him, thought Alessio, and he'll be my friend.

"Auntie!" Alessio called, entering the dining room with a bundle of books and illustrated magazines, which he hurriedly opened.

Nicolina approached the table, drying her hands on her kitchen apron. "Look what you make me do, Alessio! It's almost time for supper!" But even as she protested, she leaned over to look at the splendid illustrations with joy and curiosity.

"Just look at that avenue!"

"And this?"

"Oh, what a beautiful angel! He looks as though he could speak! Wait, Alessio, let me take a good look. Melozzo . . . His name was Melozzo? What a funny name!"

"Melozzo is the name of the painter."

"A person would be lucky to own all these beautiful things!"

"Isn't it true, auntie? My friend Rossi has a bookshelf this big, full of books and magazines."

"Get him to lend you some, a few at a time. Now that winter is coming, we'll be able to enjoy ourselves during the long evenings."

"I've also brought you a wonderful book by Turgenev. It's called *The Bread of Others*. You remember Turgenev? He's the author of *Spring Torrents*, which you liked so much. But don't show papa the books I get for you!"

"Don't worry."

"Mamma! Why don't you come and look, too?"

"I'm coming, Alessiuccio!" replied Antonietta, who had gone by carrying something into the back room. But she did not hurry. She would not have enjoyed it while standing next to her sister.

Nicolina was even forgetting her housework. In the presence of her nephew, she was recovering the joy of her adolescence, which had so quickly vanished. Gradually as Alessio was growing up, Nicolina had the illusion of living for a second time. Unwittingly he was showing her a new world, of which she had hitherto been unaware.

The books he brought her, the beautiful things he showed her, and everything he had to say about them were full of vivid revelations of a spiritual life much more lofty and noble than the shabby "everyday existence" that she dragged out as though enveloped in a gray fog. The proximity of Alessio's innocent and candid boyhood revived her closed, parched soul. He was full of feeling and enthusiasm; it took little to give him pleasure and even less to make him suffer, like a bird that warbles with joy when a ray of sunshine brightens the iron bars of its cage, and falls silent and pines away as soon as the air grows dark.

"And what's this, Alessio?"

"It's the inside of a harem. A custom of the Turks. They have more than one wife."

Don Lucio appeared in the doorway, tall, his overcoat still buttoned, rather out of sorts because no one had heard him come in. He stood looking for a moment at aunt and nephew, whose backs were turned to the door. Seen from behind, Nicolina was still quite young. Her slender neck looked powdered; her brown hair, mingling with Alessio's fine, blond hair, showed glossy reflections, like starling feathers. The vision of that youthful freshness, happy for the moment because free of care, increased his irritation. He himself was already old. Perhaps for this reason he had not shown an interest in his sister-in-law for some time.

He remained planted in the doorway, his low forehead wrinkled in a frown. He had never had such enthusiasm for looking at meaningless pictures. Grudgingly he envied their gaiety. They were enjoying themselves because they were heedless, nothing more. They had no idea of what it cost to open up a comfortable road through life, and they were reaping the fruits of his labor without paying any attention to him. They were like draft horses eating with their heads in sacks.

He thought he heard his heart beating violently, and became alarmed.

"Get rid of this stuff!" he ordered, approaching the table. "I've told you time and again not to clutter up my house with a lot of rubbish. What's more," he added, "I want you to stop pestering young Baron Rossi. One of these days his father will have reason to complain to me on your account!"

Because of his height, Don Lucio seemed to fill the room.

"I didn't hear you come in," said Nicolina apologetically. "I don't think Antonietta heard you either. She's in there."

"Go on doing as you please! Nowadays the master of the house is no more important than the cat. No one notices whether he's in or out, coming or going. Just so the boys and girls have a good time."

Alessio bundled up the books and magazines and left the room, head bowed.

Nicolina put away Don Lucio's hat, cane, and overcoat. She brought him his slippers. "Anything else you want?"

"Nothing else," Don Lucio replied in a calmer voice. Putting an arm around her waist, he bent forward a little and said to her softly, his breath on her face smelling of tobacco: "You allow your nephew too many liberties."

And since Nicolina was looking at him somewhat perplexed, he explained: "He's at a dangerous age. And you're still young yourself." His gaze, turbid with desire, was more eloquent than his brief words.

Nicolina felt the blood rush to her face. Freeing herself from the grip of his wiry arm, she ran from the room. Never had the caresses of her brother-in-law—of Alessio's father—given her such a deep feeling of disgust. She fled upstairs, collapsing on the top step, her face in her hands.

"My God! My God!" she murmured. "Is there really so much evil in the world?"

Yes, evil is everywhere, and we do not notice it and are unable to look at it. Evil is a monstrous polyp with tentacles.

"Aunt Nicolina!" cried Alessio. "Did he bawl you out because of me?"

"No, no. It has nothing to do with you!" said Nicolina brightly, drying her eyes. She looked at her nephew and smiled bitterly. His delicate face had an expression of sympathy as soft and feminine, as gentle and sad as Melozzo's angel, which they had looked at together in a moment of keen and fleeting enjoyment.

No. No. He, only he, was able to discern evil everywhere, because the evil was in his spirit.

She pressed the boy's head between her hands and kissed him tenderly on the forehead, as though she too had somehow been a mother, yes, she too, grasped forever by one of the slippery tentacles of evil.

Her ears were buzzing. Someone kept repeating (was it Antonietta? or the voice of her own heart?), someone kept repeating: "You shouldn't have stayed here . . ."

The reproach—silent and just—had ripened within her unawares. Well, she must summon the courage to make amends.

Alessio did not listen to the final instructions of Mastro Ciàula, who was renting him one of his lightest bicycles at fifty centesimi for each half hour.

He mounted the bicycle and sped away. Away through the crowded streets and finally into the open, along the sea, without catching his breath. Wildly away along the peaceful shore, past villages and farmhouses.

Away with no thought of return, happy to be racing like this, with no destination, no purpose, while the wind beat on his face with the smell of the salt sea.

Clouds filled with rosy light floated upwards from the horizon. A flock of white gulls flew over the sea. At this hour the house in the city was still in shadow; its women, the enemy sisters, were already engaged in their usual domestic chores, their thoughts frozen like a mania in the same rancor.

The sun, the strong revivifying sun, arrived late on the balconies of the sad, monotonous, oppressive house overlooking the narrow street. Outside one could breathe with joy and freedom, filling one's lungs; the mind too seemed to become open to freer and more daring thoughts . . . And one day he would escape like this, escape forever, without looking back, abandoning everything, renewing everything, like a tree renewing itself in spring.

Leaning forward over the bicycle, he had the illusion of flying. Fused with it into a single body, it was not pedals he possessed but wings! Had he perhaps suddenly become a seagull? Or one of those fabulous creatures of mythology—a winged man?

The bicycle gave a jolt. Something snapped and broke. Alessio felt himself hurled violently to one side.

A woman came running. He tried to get up, ashamed of having fallen and fearing he had ruined a bicycle that didn't belong to him. Some fishermen who were repairing nets on the sand, a passing workman, approached.

"He didn't see the ditch . . ."

"He was racing like mad, like mad!"

"I tried to yell at him!"

Alessio couldn't walk. His leg hurt, and he sat down disheartened.

"It's busted, signorino," said the workman, inspecting the bicycle. "It's really finished. Going to have to replace the part. But wait a minute! Holy saints!" he exclaimed, taking a closer look. "It's been welded right here, see? Right at this point! And you were going so fast! Didn't you know about it?"

"It's a rented bicycle," Alessio confessed, taking a look himself.

An old weld was visible at the break. This cheered him up somewhat. Mastro Ciàula could hardly insist on being paid.

He started back on foot, dejected because his leg still hurt. He was exhausted when he reached Mastro Ciàula's, who greeted him by saying: "That was two hours, not half an hour. You owe me two lire."

On examining the break, his face turned as dark as midnight. He answered Alessio's justifications by shouting and throwing his cap on the ground.

"Tricked! Tricked!" he repeated, guffawing. "Nobody's tricked you! You can go to hell! The bicycle was in perfect condition. No? So why didn't you look at it first? Mastro Ciàulo doesn't cheat people. He's a honest man. Ask anyone you like. If this bicycle had been ridden by someone with any sense, it wouldn't be broken now."

Then he calmed down, and putting his cap back on his head, said firmly: "It's going to cost you fifty lire to have it fixed: it needs a whole new part. And two lire for renting it, that makes fifty-two. You can bring me the money tomorrow. I'll even give you till the day after tomorrow. Tell your papa. Aren't you the son of Don Lucio Carmine? He's got the money to pay for it. You can be sure of that! Just what Don Lucio Carmine needed—a son like you!"

Alessio felt his blood run cold. Dejected, he made his way home, his head drooping between his shoulders. Seen from outside, the house, larger and darker than usual, looked almost frightening.

"Where are you coming from so late? Haven't you been to school? What have you done to yourself? All muddy! All dusty!"

"Nothing. Be quiet. I fell down. Is papa back?"

"Not yet."

As he hurried up the stairs, he heard Nicolina's voice saying loudly: "Nobody. Alessio's back."

It seemed to him that Nicolina had a new or at least different voice from her usual one. She had said something simple and correct, something he had never thought of. Nobody . . . He was "nobody." His grief was multiplied, without his knowing why.

He waited for his father to start smoking his pipe after the ample breakfast, knowing that then he wouldn't stir even if the house were to collapse.

He confided to his mother the trouble he was in. "You have to find a way to tell him," he concluded. "You'll be able to do it better than I. To me he won't listen. The important thing is that before paying, he should make him understand that I'm right. It's blackmail. Mastro Ciàula is taking advantage of me because I'm a kid. Papa can straighten things out."

Antonietta was alarmed. Fifty lire! Fifty lire!

"After all," added Alessio, and a shadow crossed his

face, "it's not the end of the world, is it? It's just a matter of showing that man that I'm not an orphan and that when the time comes, I have a father who'll back me up. Because right is on my side."

Antonietta remained perplexed for a moment. Finally, out of love for her son, she got up her courage. "Wait," she whispered.

She went into the dining room, hesitating a moment. She closed the door. She approached the table. "Lucio," she said at last. "I must speak to you."

Don Lucio, frowning, raised his eyes. It would certainly be about that old woman in Sant'Agata. He was getting sick and tired of her.

"Alessio," Antonietta began, "went for a ride on a bicycle yesterday. A rented one, of course. To get some exercise. He fell and hurt himself. The bicycle got broken a little. I mean, a lot. It got broken," she repeated, without concealing her embarrassment, and not knowing how to go on. "An important piece of the bicycle broke, I don't know what it's called."

Alessio listened in chagrin. Was all this preamble really necessary? Not that he wouldn't have put it just as badly himself! But a wife is not a son and she can permit herself a few clearer, more concise words! She ought to have explained the matter in a few sentences. It was so obvious that right was on his side! The money was secondary.

His mother's subdued, almost plaintive tone of voice tore his soul. Oh, why are we all such cowards in this house? he wondered, exasperated.

"They tricked him, poor boy. Now he's brought back the bicycle and they want fifty lire," Antonietta said finally, all in one breath.

"And what does all this mess have to do with me?" said Don Lucio in his phlegmatic tone that was sometimes crueler than a whiplash.

"My God!" whispered Antonietta, twisting her chilled hands under her black apron. "Obviously he has to turn to you for help. Where else can the poor boy go?"

"To me? He's starting early to throw money away, that young man. Fifty lire! Fifty lire," he repeated calmly, setting his pipe on the copper tray, "doesn't grow on trees. I don't have the money to pay for his foolishness. I work. Time and again I've forbidden him to rent bicycles."

"So what am I to tell that poor child, waiting like a soul in torment?"

Nicolina was listening in the kitchen with bated breath. She had been on the point of entering to add her voice to Antonietta's, but had stayed where she was for fear of making things worse.

"Tell him," replied Don Lucio, finally looking his wife in the face, while she trembled as though stricken with tertian fever, "tell him to learn to obey. And you, don't keep standing there like a hopeless case. All I get from your son are bitter pills to swallow."

Antonietta left the room. Nicolina was crying silently near the stove.

Softly, so that Don Lucio wouldn't hear, the mother said to her son, "Look, he doesn't have it just now. But don't worry. You'll see, by four o'clock I and . . . your aunt, we'll find the money. Anyway it's not a big sum."

"I heard," said Alessio with a smile so desolate it wrung his mother's heart. "It's not right that you should start worrying yourselves on *my* account too.

I'll go and ask Ferdinando, you know, my rich friend at school. I'll pay him back a little at a time. Papa doesn't have to know anything about it. I can count on Rossi. He's like a brother to me."

"Yes, that's what we'll do," Antonietta exclaimed, reassured. "That's a really good idea, Alessio. But where are you going at this hour? You said there was no school today."

"I've checked the schedule. I have an hour of math. After that I'll go see Ferdinando Rossi. Listen," he added, hugging his mother and hiding his face on her shoulder. "Forgive me if I've given you all this trouble. And be brave. Be brave, mamma. Life is sad. And please forgive Aunt Nicolina. She's suffered, too. So that's all . . ." And he tried to smile so as not to give undue gravity to the words that came spontaneously from the depths of his heart. It was the first time he had dared to mention "that matter." His mother gave a start.

"You're crying?" she exclaimed, stepping back to look him in the face.

"I feel sort of funny this morning," said Alessio, smiling again, his chin trembling a little. "Give me your blessing, mamma."

"God bless you, my son."

Alessio cautiously opened the door. Don Lucio was having his hair combed; with his head resting against the back of the chair, he seemed to be dozing. Nicolina was combing him slowly. Her eyes were red.

Steadily and sluggishly as always, the hours kept passing in the house in the shadows. Alessio waved goodbye to Nicolina and disappeared swiftly down the damp, dark stairs.

*   *   *

101

Don Lucio, already at the table, clinked his knife against the bottle as a sign of impatience. Then Antonietta with both hands picked up the tureen, which had been ready for some time, and Nicolina warmed her brother-in-law's plate so that his soup would be served hot.

Alessio was really getting to be a pain! And to think he was still just a boy! After the incident of the morning he had gone out and no one had seen him since. Where had he gone? Where was he keeping himself at this hour?

And what if his friend refuses to help him? thought Antonietta as she set down the soup tureen.

"How long has he been gone?" Don Lucio asked after a silence, while Antonietta ladled out the soup and the little girls hastily crossed themselves.

No one answered. When Don Lucio repeated his idle question, Antonietta murmured, "Since this morning. As you know."

Don Lucio began eating. The silence hung in the room like fog. The girls scooped up the last spoonfuls of soup, trying not to make noise. Even Antonietta was impatient to finish, to get up, and go to the window and wait for Alessio.

Only Don Lucio did not lose his calm: with his shoulders resting comfortably on the back of the leather armchair, his eyes half closed, he chewed slowly, savoring his food.

Finally the little girls were allowed to leave the table. Antonietta cleared it. Nicolina brought the coffee pot to the table, along with everything else that was needed, since Don Lucio liked to watch her prepare the coffee and to smell its aroma. Nicolina looked calm as she carried out her task with her usual precision. She ground the coffee, put a spoonful in the steaming jug, covered it, stirred it as soon as it came to a boil, covered it again, and finally extinguished the flame without a drop of water being spilled or a spot of black foam staining the clean shining jug, which looked like silver.

But like Antonietta, she was gripped with apprehension. No, it had never happened that Alessio was so late in coming home!

Don Lucio sipped his coffee voluptuously. Satiated, well satisfied, he desired nothing at that moment, and in his heart had completely forgotten his son's absence. Nor did he notice the anxiety that had turned the faces of the two women pale.

There was a knock at the door. A discreet, almost timid knock. No doubt it was Alessio. He would come in, as usual somewhat excited, somewhat anxious. Carmelina ran to open the door.

"Papa, someone wants to speak to you."

"At this hour!" snorted Don Lucio. "Tell him . . . No. Come back here," he corrected himself immediately, putting down his cup in annoyance, remembering a borrower who wanted to see him.

The women listened. They heard a confused, disconnected whispering, then the door being closed and the bedroom door being opened. "Antonietta!" Don Lucio called.

They both ran to him.

"I have to go out."

They helped him put on his overcoat; then they tried to adjust his necktie, but Don Lucio was in a hurry.

"Never mind, never mind . . ." he said. His voice had never sounded so strange. In his agitation, he kept looking for things without saying what he wanted, and his hands were trembling. Antonietta got up her courage and went back, unseen, to the vestibule.

Something had happened that concerned her too. She felt it. The man was still standing before the closed door, his head lowered, his cap in his hands—a braided cap. Antonietta guessed that he was a servant of Baron Rossi.

Softly, hurriedly, she said to him: "For the love of God, tell me what's happened, if it's something . . ." She wanted to say "if it's something that has to do with me," but her voice trailed off in anxiety, because she was thinking of Alessio, only of Alessio.

The servant, seeing her so upset, thought she knew. "Don't be frightened," he replied. "It's not serious."

Antonietta stared at him, her eyes wide and dilated. "What's not serious? Speak plainly. My son hasn't come home since this morning. Have pity on a mother. Tell me where he is."

The servant, perplexed in his turn, looked at her without knowing how to behave, since he had been given strict orders. But he felt sorry for the poor lady who looked so upset and was waiting for him to speak, and as Don Lucio came out of the bedroom, wrapped in his woolen scarf against the cold of the night, he whispered, "I'm from the Rossi household, as you can see. Take heart, signora."

Antonietta felt a sharp, rending pain, as though they had ripped her stomach. "Lucio! Lucio!" she cried, running after her husband.

He turned around brusquely, motioning to her to keep quiet and stay in the house. "I'm coming right back," he shouted. And he continued down the stairs.

Antonietta remained on the landing as though petrified.

"Who was it? What's happened?" Nicolina kept saying.

"It's Baron Rossi's servant. The Madonna has punished us."

And she collapsed on the landing like a bundle of rags. Nicolina thrust her hands into her hair.

"Alessio! Alessiuccio!" she murmured desperately. She saw the stairs wobble and whirl, as though she were on a ship, and her ears were ringing.

Both of them remained silent for a moment. The little girls, frightened at seeing their mother lying on the floor outside the door, began to cry, and Nicolina, hearing them, gave a start. "Keep quiet," she scolded them. "What's the meaning of this crying? It just brings bad luck. Keep quiet. We don't know anything yet." And in a lower voice, grasping at a straw, she added, "Maybe he doesn't have the courage to come home at this hour."

She bent over Antonietta. "Get up," she urged gently.

"No!" her sister exclaimed, without looking at her. "Let me wait in peace."

They were silent again, remaining outside the door like two beggars. And the minutes, passing in a silence weighed down by mystery and fear, were eternal.

"That was Baron Rossi's servant," Nicolina said finally, and it sounded as though she were talking in her sleep. "Antonietta, I know where the baron lives."

Then Antonietta struggled to her feet, giving her hand to her sister. "The Madonna has punished us," she repeated.

The look on her face was like that of a weak and wounded man who must accept the help of his hated enemy.

The crowd, dense as a hedge, pressed around the closed portal of the mansion. Newcomers kept arriving in the square: some stopped to ask what had happened, others hurried away, not wishing to be called to testify in case some crime had been committed.

A woman wept, repeating over and over: "At that age! At that age! Lord, hold your hands over the heads of my children!"

An old gentleman, with gold-rimmed spectacles and a long white beard, also stopped to ask.

"He was a happy boy," explained a wizened little man (it was the notary Marullo). "An only son, adored by his parents. They gave him everything . . ."

"Eh! Eh!" The old gentleman gave a discreet cough. "Who knows what goes on in their minds, my dear notary? You can torment a child without meaning to and without knowing it. There's a certain age when the little miseries of life seem terrible. They get magnified out of all proportion. If we only paid a little more attention to them . . ."

Whereupon the old man walked away. A workman wanted to have his say:

"That's a lot of fancy talk from that gentleman. Well, I may not be able to read or write, but I know something about life. I know that it's these times that are to blame. Such things didn't use to happen. Children didn't go around asking for the moon. They just wanted to eat and sleep, and were only afraid of their fathers. Nowadays they're old before they're born . . ."

106

A murmur ran through the crowd. A tall thin man in an overcoat was crossing the square, followed by a servant.

"It's the father," they whispered.

"That one?"

"Yes, that one."

"I recognized the servant who went to call him."

"Give me a little room. I can't see him!"

"It's the father . . ."

"It's the father. . ." the crowd kept whispering, pressing closer to the portal, which opened to let Don Lucio in, and immediately swung heavily shut. Through the crowd, like a shiver, ran a morbid curiosity to witness the scene going on above, in the lighted room.

The portal opened again and closed. The servant emerged with a note. He was stopped. There were still people who hadn't heard all the details.

"I know nothing about it," the servant kept saying, moved, and unable to overcome the need he felt to unburden himself and talk about it. "My poor young master has been put to bed, he's had such a shock. The doctor is with him. The same doctor who was called for the 'other one.' I'm running to get some medicine. I'm in a hurry. Let me through. How did it happen? I know nothing about it. My young master says his friend wanted to try the gun, as a joke, after lunch. That's what he told the police. It's the truth. He had stayed for lunch with us because he'd decided, 'I'm not going back home.' The baron promised to speak to his father. 'You'll see, everything's going to be all right.' He didn't want him to. First he was excited. He himself didn't know what he wanted to do. He wanted to run away. He talked of stowing away on a ship. I heard him myself, he was talking nonsense. That was why the young baron wanted to stay close to him. He loved him as though they were equals. It looked as though he'd been able to calm him down. It would have been better if they'd let him go! By this time, who knows? Then he wanted to try the gun. He said, 'Lucky you, you even have a revolver within reach!' My young master burst out laughing. Then they started reading a book. While they were reading, my young master had to go into his grandfather the old baron's study. He left the other one alone. He'd sometimes leave him alone because, he says, he was so well brought up he didn't even dare look at the books in a bookstore. So he goes. It wasn't a minute later when he heard a shot . . . then another. You can see that all of a sudden an awful idea must have gone through his head. Like a storm. Our minds are like the bottom of the sea. If my young master hadn't left him alone, with that revolver within reach . . . Who knows! Once the moment had passed . . . From that room you can go directly into the garden. He went into the garden. What a business, I tell you, what a business! O Lord, to see him now! He doesn't look as though he'd died a violent death! Let me go through, for heaven's sake, they're waiting for the medicine . . ."

He went on his way, still talking to himself and gesticulating. The crowd began to break up, since there was nothing more to see or hear.

Two women, wrapped in black shawls, moved across the half-deserted square. They knocked and went inside.

Even the few remaining spectators dispersed. The spectacle was over. The Rossi mansion, dark and majestic, stood isolated, shut tight. A single window remained open, filled by the flickering red glow of lighted torches.

During the three days of visits, the little girls were left with the nuns even overnight. Don Lucio—unshaven, his cap pulled down to his ears, with all the look of a man in mourning—commiserated with himself by glancing in the mirror, and in his free moments went to whip up some eggs in the kitchen, since it seemed to him that his pulse was beating rather feebly.

For three days there was a procession of callers. Don Lucio had many friends and acquaintances: members of the clubs and leagues to which he belonged, people employed by the baron, and, most of all, debtors.

Some came out of duty, some with the hope of ingratiating themselves with him, some out of curiosity, some for the pleasure of finally being allowed to set foot in the house of a man who, without being a misanthrope, had never shown any desire to open his door to anyone.

All these visits reassured Don Lucio and gradually freed him from the haunting fear that Alessio's violent death might be a blot on the good reputation he had built for himself in the city. In those very days the baron had promised to entrust to him, him alone, the entire administration of his property, and the assessor Laurà had held out the hope of an appointment in City Hall. Everyone esteemed him, appreciated him, flattered him. But would not his enemies, waiting in the shadows to stab him in the back, make use of this tragic event to call attention to his private life, and discredit him with the baron and with anyone else who had faith in him?

These thoughts nagged him. But little by little his fears dissipated. The boy had left nothing that might have explained his frightful decision—which perhaps had come over him suddenly like a fit of madness. He hadn't written a word. His notebooks and school books, left neatly piled on the little table at the foot of Nicolina's bed, contained no sign. He had gone away just like that, leaving no trace of himself.

The visitors entered the darkened parlor unannounced and sat down in silence, as is the custom.

"A blow . . . a heavy blow . . . Courage, my poor friend . . ."

In low voices they wove their praises, reiterating that a man like him, devoted to his family as he was, did not deserve such a terrible misfortune. Don Lucio, sunk in an armchair, his chin on his chest, seemed not to be listening, as is the custom.

There was even an article in *Scilla e Cariddi*. Someone passed it on to Don Lucio, with a significant look.

"For when you're feeling calmer. It's by a teacher at the high school. It's written with a lot of insight."

In subdued tones he summarized the contents of the article, which spoke of the decadence of the times, and the unsettling books being read by young people. Don Lucio took the newspaper without saying a word and placed it on the table beside his chair, where the condolences were displayed: notes from acquaintances, a telegram from his married sisters in Catania, a letter from Sant'Agata, and, most conspicuously, a note in the baron's handwriting, and an envelope with the City Hall seal, from the assessor Laurà. It was good that his enemies, if there were any among the visitors, should see that Don Lucio Carmine, even in misfortune, was still a man of some importance.

He listened with interest to the various comments, descriptions, and brief observations, which gave him an idea of the impression aroused in the city. Everyone looked on the sad event in the same way. They seemed to speak with one voice.

Alessio was judged with indulgence, as a youngster ruined by reading unsuitable books. Public opinion and the brilliant psychological article in *Scilla e Cariddi* were confirmed by the fact that a book entitled *Life Is a Bagatelle* had been found lying open on the table where the two young friends had been sitting and reading.

The women, holed up in the dining room, received no visits. They knew no one. Only a few women neighbors on the street and the widow from the first floor came up out of compassion for the two poor ladies, "alone like souls in torment."

On one of the three evenings the wife of a clerk who had borrowed a large sum from Don Lucio also came. The clerk had had the idea of bringing his wife along, in the hope that by this homage his overdue debt might be forgiven.

She was a badly dressed lady, wearing a shabby silk shawl that had turned rusty with age. As long as her visit lasted—she was waiting for her husband in the parlor to come and fetch her—she kept silent, her hands folded and her eyes on the floor: poor hands that one imagined as twisted and gnarled, inside her coarse cotton gloves; tired eyes, with slightly reddened eyelids. Her presence brought a kind of comfort to the shadow-filled room. She did not speak. But she seemed to say softly, by her humble and resigned attitude as a poor woman:

"It's our life. What can we do about it? That's the way things are. Working, raising our children in pain. We give our babies milk, and a few tears that drop from our eyelashes. It's those tears, sucked in with the milk, that poison their lives forever . . ."

And the women, absorbed, bowing their heads a little, seemed to approve the unspoken words.

A moment before leaving, the clerk's wife did speak, almost as though she were resuming an interrupted discourse:

". . . my daughter was fifteen years old when she ran away from home. Now finally we've made up. But her husband beats her and she works to support him. Many nights we hear someone knocking. I go and open the door. There she is, coming to take refuge in our house. That's why my husband's pension isn't enough. Now, I ask you, wouldn't it have been better to mourn her once and for all, instead of watching her drag out such a miserable existence?"

She fell silent, wiping her eyes. What she meant was that there are times when death is wiser than life.

The two sisters looked at her for a moment. Silence again filled the room.

Antonietta had not wept once. Her eyes had remained dry even when entering the strange house where Alessio lay; now her eyes burned as though all her unshed tears lay clotted in her eyelashes.

Nicolina was tired, enervated. Twice she had fainted. Now, her head heavy, she was yawning. She could hear the monotonous murmuring from the parlor. Time dragged on. She was suffering, as though waiting for a release that was taking forever to come, and every so often she looked imploringly at her sister.

But Antonietta sat motionless, huddled in the shadows. Her face, emerging from her black shawl as from a dark oval frame, had yellowish reflections. She stared straight ahead, without blinking. Nicolina was afraid of that expressionless face. In the darkness, amid the soft folds of the black shawl, it looked disembodied, like the apparition of a ghost. She lit the lamp so she could see her sister, and not merely that suspended face.

Antonietta stood up. She didn't want the light. She went and huddled in the farthest corner, where she resumed her motionless pose. And again Nicolina saw emerging from the shadow a face that looked like that of a dead woman rising from the water of a ghastly swamp.

Exasperated, she covered her eyes with her hands. Her eyes closed, she again saw her dead nephew, lying on his rich friend's bed, between two large flaming and smoking torches. Then she wept with terror, softly, like a little girl pursued by her own shadow and who finds no escape.

God! My God! Would it always be like this? Like this? Always? And she moaned and sobbed aloud to break the silence in the room, hoping that Antonietta too would vent herself in tears.

But Antonietta remained impassive.

Nicolina prepared the lemon water. She brought the briefcase to the table. She looked around to make sure that everything was in place, that her brother-in-law would find everything he wanted when he returned. Now he had started taking a walk after supper. Perhaps the evenings seemed long to him, too.

She paused before the closed door of the bedroom. "Goodnight, Antonietta. I'm going to bed," she called. She stood for a moment, waiting for a response to come through the door. She went up the wooden staircase, relieved by the certainty that for that evening she would not have to meet her brother-in-law. She was still the meek and obedient Nicolina. But now she resisted him.

"Leave me alone," she had the courage to beg hoarsely, when he seized her by both wrists, pulling her to his chest. "Leave me alone . . ."

He let her go and frowning, watched her leave the room, frail, slender, her shoulders rather full and her chest hollow, her hips barely showing under the wide skirt of black calico. He too, for a moment, again saw Alessio on the strange bed in the strange house, looking as calm as if he had unwittingly fallen asleep. He took off his glasses, and sinking back in the leather armchair, began to smoke so as to stop seeing such things. But he was not always able to erase the painful vision. He went out. He hoped he might meet some friend who would invite him to a café or the theater, or at least force him to walk for a while and converse.

He surely had the right to live in peace. He'd done no harm to anyone. The fate of things wasn't in his hands. Naturally, had it been in his power, he would have made his son happy.

But what on earth had that boy been suffering from? Had he perhaps mistreated him? Had he been a tyrannical father, a cold-hearted father?

His own childhood, yes, had been harsh and bitter! He had been raised by his grandfather, a strong and capricious old man, who had beaten him unmercifully, and later had thrown him out of the house. Well, he had found in himself the strength and means to make his own way. Even his sisters, poor but resigned and cautious, had found their way in life.

The "other one"—his son—had been a weakling. A refusal (and Don Lucio winced at the memory as though someone in his own soul were accusing him), a refusal bluntly delivered for his own good, had been enough to derange his mind and make life seem a burden to him.

He had been a weakling. Soon he would have been defeated. No, it was not his fault if he'd been unable to transmit to him whole the energetic will to live.

With these thoughts, these efforts to convince himself, he recovered his self-mastery.

Then, when disgust with his speculations overcame him—thinking of the incident of the gold necklace—he became harsher with his debtors and did not bother to be secretive at home.

"Yes," he said to Nicolina, who was looking fearfully at the fine pieces of jewelry in the ebony box. "Yes, that's what I do with my money. The girls will be rich someday. I do it for them. But don't you be stupid too! Do you think I'm the sort of man to ruin people? Do I look like a pawnbroker? It's a business like any other . . ."

No. He couldn't allow the memory of Alessio, the shock of *that* evening at Christmas, above all the false sense of decorum he had hitherto nourished, to paralyze his will.

115

And he sought every opportunity to instill fear in his daughters—wan, tall and gawky, dressed in black. So that they wouldn't elude him like Alessio, he had stopped sending them to the nuns. He meant to keep an eye on them. He intended to raise them himself, in his own way, to be docile, simple, ignorant, and without wishes, the way women should be.

Sometimes in the evening, when the girls had gone to bed and Nicolina was still moving around the house, he called her. He would put his arms around her, kissing the nape of her neck with violence, almost with rage, to establish once again that he was the master.

"Leave me alone . . ." she protested, reluctant, her face blanching.

And she found the strength to put up a struggle and defend herself. He paid no attention. He enjoyed overcoming her, and showing who was the stronger. Holding her tightly, he led her into the small sitting room—where he now slept alone—with a wicked smile under his toothbrush moustache. He could feel Nicolina trembling in his sinewy arms. But he chose to pay no attention.

Those nights, while her sleeping brother-in-law snored, Nicolina kept vigil. Sitting at the foot of her unrumpled cot, beside the little table on which Alessio's books were still neatly stacked, she kept vigil and prayed. And she prayed for her brother-in-law as well, and asked forgiveness for him.

Though it seemed much the same, life had changed irrevocably for all of them. Even Don Lucio became aware of it. His sister-in-law continued to wait on him with the same punctuality, but her pale, doleful face bore the resigned expression of one who is fulfilling an unpleasant obligation. Antonietta did not leave her room unless summoned. She would gaze stubbornly at Don Lucio, as though she wanted to speak to him but didn't dare. Her mute and sorrowing presence was extremely irritating to her husband, who finally suggested that they stop calling her at mealtimes.

"You can see she'd rather be alone," he concluded to justify his suggestion, which had been uttered in a tone so curt that it sounded like a command.

The girls set up a small table in the bedroom and brought her her meals. Antonietta, who had arranged a peculiar little altar next to her bed, thanked the Lord in her prayers, happy that her husband was finally leaving her in peace in her little refuge. She took no notice of anything, she was not interested in anything. Only her daughters still caught her attention.

"Does Aunt Nicolina love you?" she asked them. "Are you happy? I thank you, Lord. You see, I can't do anything for you. The Madonna will be your little mamma and she'll take care of you. If only I'd asked her to take care of Alessiuccio! Because, you see, we can't foresee good or prevent evil . . ."

She ate very little. She no longer undressed to go to bed, but would doze for an hour or so in front of her altar. Her gaze became as fixed as her thought.

She was becoming stupefied.

As time went on, Don Lucio began to worry about Antonietta's condition. Perhaps they ought to change their way of life, at least for the time being. He was ready to sacrifice himself, give up all his habits, spend money recklessly, so that life might finally begin again *as before*, renewed and freed from the cloud that hung over them all. The purpose of money is to provide for our well-being! He was not a miser, piling up coins for the pleasure of it. He had never minded the expense when it came to surrounding himself with comforts and making his days agreeable.

He decided to talk to Nicolina, since she seemed more reasonable than her sister and because he didn't like to speak directly to his wife about *that*. Ever since the evening when they had found themselves face to face in a room in the Rossi mansion, they had never had a conversation.

"Sit down," he said solemnly. And he began slowly lighting his pipe, while his sister-in-law waited, her hands in her lap, her expression meek and downcast.

"I've been thinking," he said finally, after blowing out a few puffs of smoke. "You look exhausted. A change of air would do you good."

And since Nicolina seemed neither to understand or show any interest, he added: "It's six years since you've been to Sant'Agata. Your mother is getting on. I'll give you permission and money for the trip."

Nicolina raised her eyes to his. "No," she replied. "I'm not going."

Don Lucio thought he understood his sister-in-law's rapid reasoning and explained with unaccustomed placidity in his voice: "I don't mean just you. Antonietta too. And the girls. You'll all have a good time."

Nicolina bowed her head. Her eyes filled with hot tears at the fear of having to leave (was this what her brother-in-law wanted?), of having to leave perhaps forever. It was not the house she loved—far from it!—but the painful and bitter memories that swarmed there, forming part of her past, of her very life.

To have to leave, now that there was nothing for

118

which to have to make amends ... Better if I killed myself like him, she thought. But she also thought of Antonietta, and felt a bitter consolation.

"Antonietta won't want to," she said, and stood up since she had nothing more to add.

Don Lucio looked at her in surprise. He finished smoking his pipe and then went resolutely into his wife's bedroom. It had to be done.

Antonietta was knitting beside the window. Hearing her husband come in, she put aside her work and waited calmly. Don Lucio sat down and, in the same words, told his wife what he had told his sister-in-law.

"Why do you want to send me away?" Antonietta asked softly.

Don Lucio pretended to lose his temper. He shouted that he was thinking of the well-being of others and that all that he got in return was ingratitude. He knew he would accomplish much more by demanding than by asking.

"Don't you see that this life is unbearable? I made that clear to Nicolina. But she insists on staying too."

Antonietta gave a sigh of relief. Even her sister, her enemy, agreed with her. Here they were once again in accord, without even speaking to each other. The bond that united them, for life and death, was still stronger than the jealousy that divided them even in grief.

Now Don Lucio really lost his temper. He paced back and forth in the room, pouring out everything he had vainly tried to suppress for fear of getting ill.

"No," he repeated hoarsely, "your and your sister's accusing looks don't scare me. Is it my fault? Answer me! Take this burden off me. Are you really both accusing me? It's not my fault. I did my duty. I did nothing, absolutely nothing to make him suffer, but he was a weakling . . ." His anger subsided slowly in these final words, which echoed in the room like sobs.

Antonietta listened to him, without getting frightened. He could no longer hurt her.

Then she said, and her voice was calm: "So what are you worried about? It wasn't your fault and it wasn't mine. Not even mine. If only I'd understood, how everything made him suffer . . . Because now I understand it. I remember so many things, they come back clearly to my mind, each one like an explanation. He was hurt by the dissension in our home. All of us poisoned his life a little, the way a fresh spring gets poisoned. If only I'd understood, I would have taken him away. The world is wide. I would have found a refuge for the two of us, to make him forget the evil he'd had a glimpse of. But I didn't understand. Now it's too late for me to go away. Now that he's not here any more. Without meaning to, we killed him, and yet we all think we're not to blame. Don't get angry, Lucio. You see, we all carry the burden of our own fate on our backs. He was too frail to walk to the end with his burden. Yes," she repeated, as though speaking in a dream, "we all killed him a little, without meaning to. Don't get angry. That's the way it is. Once, back home, I had a goldfinch. It was very tame. It fluttered around the house, and would sit on my shoulder. One day they were calling me and I opened a door. The little bird got crushed. It wasn't the fault of whoever was calling me, and it wasn't mine for opening the door. Could we always go around thinking that we had a tiny bird in the house? That's the way it is. We all forgot there was a creature who understood and suffered. Don't get angry, Lucio. It's no use."

120

But Don Lucio was no longer angry. He was upset by the excessively calm tone of her voice. She was reasoning quietly as though discussing something completely foreign to her. This was the way he had once heard a madman talk. In the pale, flaccid face, the dilated eyes glowed without expression.

"Shall we do something?" he said gently, as though speaking to a sick child. "Shall we send Nicolina to Sant'Agata for a while?"

His wife looked at him, upset in her turn. "No," she begged. "Alessio wouldn't like it. Just last night he said to me, 'Mamma, don't send your sister away.' "

"Then . . . But listen! Be reasonable!" exclaimed Don Lucio in a tone of command. "Nicolina will take the girls with her. I . . . we . . . we'll go someplace else. To my sisters in Catania. Or to Patti, where the baron owns land. You'll enjoy it. I don't care about the expense. And life—" he added, almost bashfully, lowering his voice "—will start over again for us all."

"Don't send me away, Lucio!" Antonietta implored. "How could you be so mean as to want to keep me from mourning him? I don't give you any trouble, shut up in here."

She fell silent. And her whole person assumed the downcast attitude of Nicolina.

At that moment the two sisters resembled each other. They were also thinking the same things. Yet they would never approach each other, never exchange a word of comfort.

Don Lucio thought of the time when they were girls in Sant'Agata, holding each other's hands, dressed in the same color, and looking at each other with the same gentle expression of love and devotion.

121

So much talking had made Antonietta tired and distraught. She raised her bewildered eyes.

"Go away!" she said. "When you people are here, he won't come in. He's so beautiful! He comes and stands beside me and talks to me. Please go away . . ."

She smiled. That foolish smile on the distraught face frightened Don Lucio, and he hurried, almost fled, from the bedroom.

In the hallway he felt out of breath. The floor swayed under his feet. He leaned against the wall.

There was something that eluded his will. There was someone (not his wife, not others . . .), someone voiceless and without gestures, who was thwarting him for the first time.

But he, he alone, had to be the stronger. He went into the dining room. He sat down in his usual place, holding both hands on his chest to feel the beating of his heart.

To get emotional and have arguments after having eaten? Too often he forgot he was sick. He compressed his lips, terrified at the sharp, relentless pang in his heart.

One ought to take life as it came. Relax, go out more often, be sociable. It's hygienic to exchange a few words with an acquaintance, have a chat about unimportant things, after one's meals.

He had also joined Humanitas (the league for the protection of young girls) and they had given him the sensitive post in City Hall (the one promised by the assessor Laurà). He had plenty to do outside the house. He couldn't let his brains get addled like a silly woman.

He stood up and went to get dressed to go out. In the vestibule Nicolina helped him put on his coat and brushed his lapels. But the solicitude with which his sister-in-law—thin, pale, dressed in black—surrounded him gave him no satisfaction.

He went down the stairs very slowly, deeply worried by the recurring pang. He could die at any time, go out of the house never to return.

No, one had to start living again, as before.

He set out slowly. For a moment his wavering shadow loomed large on the poorly lighted street.

And life began anew, with its identical days. The house on the side street, regulated like clockwork, seemed filled with peace, as before. Each person resumed the old habits, which were followed mechanically, like the movements of a hand as it sews. They all lived for themselves, with a great solitude in their souls; alien, indifferent to those who breathed the same air and cut the same bread, like people who live in the same hotel without knowing each other.

Now the violet evening descends on the shadow-filled side street, softening the light that still shines here and there over the boundless expanse of roofs, as far as the distant vermilion and orange horizon.

Antonietta is in her room. She hardly understands any more what they say to her, and in the house they have resigned themselves to this new but bearable punishment. In the twilight, beside the closed window, she goes on knitting and talking to the holy images, which she sees as kindly and beloved persons who have not betrayed her.

Nicolina is in her own little room in the garret. No one needs her at this hour. She sews and thinks. Her thoughts are bitter, like a lump of tears that she cannot succeed in shedding. Since the evening is sultry, she has left the window open: the little round window, out of which she and Alessio had peered so many times. In the lonely room, his youthful voice still seems to ring out:

"Look, auntie! Right now the room is the cabin of a ship that's about to leave port."

The whole house, the old ship rotting in the port, full of travelers who have never seen the broad horizon, is soon wrapped in the shadows of night. No room has a lighted lamp. Don Lucio is out. When he returns, he will be seen sitting at the table in the dining room, under the round beam of the hanging lamp, which sways a little if a footstep crosses the room.

"Agata!" he will call. "Tell Aunt Nicolina to fill my pipe."

The two girls linger on the terrace, where Aunt Nicolina used to sit. How can they go to bed when the air is so warm and they aren't sleepy?

They hold each other by the hand and say nothing. What they think, and what swells their young hearts, which on calm summer evenings beat like leaves caressed by the wind, is too soft and vague, and they have no idea how to express it.

"Look at all the stars in the sky!" Agata exclaims. "Let's see if we can count them."

And they try to count them. And then fall silent. There is a sudden aroma of flowers. It must be from some nearby garden. A sound . . . Maybe it comes from the wider street over there.

"Doesn't it seem like we can smell the sea?" says Agata.

"Hush!" exclaims Carmelina, who always thinks of

Alessio when anyone mentions the sea. They listen. A footstep, a voice in the street. An impetuous exuberance surges in their young bosoms. They are growing up like certain odd delicate flowers that appear between the cracks in old walls and that the rain will soon spoil. Don Lucio clears his throat. The two girls are startled, but then laugh for having been startled; and then they are silent, once again waiting, anxious and moved, while the heavy, silent hours pass across the starry sky.

AFTERWORD

MARIA MESSINA—Aunt Maria to us children—was scarcely more than twenty years old when, in 1909, she began publishing her first books. The only experience of life she had came from observing with precocious eyes the closed environment of the small Sicilian province in which she lived.

We, her nieces, daughters of her only brother, knew nothing about her or her life. Children, after all, are more interested in fairies, dragons, and the adventures of Prince Charming than in the lives of real people. We knew our aunt was a writer, and when we went to visit our grandparents it was a joy to listen to the fairy tales she told us and which we would afterwards rediscover at home in the beautifully bound volumes that we used to leaf through even before we knew how to read. But it was only later, much later, that I knew anything about her unhappy childhood, and her humiliated adolescence in the shadow of a painful family situation.

My grandparents' marriage had not been a happy one. She was a girl from a noble family, but plain-looking and without a penny of dowry. Her father, one of the last representatives of the Sicilian nobility that was still living in complete feudalism at the beginning of the twentieth century, had squandered his whole inheritance on baccarat and roulette, and could hardly wait to get this almost unmarriageable daughter off his hands. The opportunity came when a student from Palermo turned up by chance in that provincial town. My grandmother, who was romantic (and how could a sixteen-year-old girl just out of boarding school and with her head full of dreams not be romantic?), fell in love with the handsome youth she had glimpsed from the window. And he, flattered at first by the infatuation of a girl so much above him by birth, found himself trapped, without even knowing how it had happened, in a marriage he hadn't wanted. Not being rich himself, he was forced to interrupt his studies and take on a modest job as an elementary-school teacher in order to support his family.

The marriage that had begun so badly worsened as time went on, between misunderstandings and economic privations for which neither of the two had been prepared. And their children suffered from it.

In Sicily in those days the "male child" had ways to escape, if he wanted to, from the narrowness of provincial life: he could study, go out with his friends and sow his wild oats, go to the university, and finally have a career and independence. But for a girl, confined to embroidery and piano lessons, there was no other hope but a marriage arranged by her family, or if she was lucky one that might blossom amid family reunions and parties, which were strictly overseen by her parents. In that joyless house, whose poverty had to be decorously concealed, even this was lacking, and Maria would have withered like a spring without sun had not her brother, who was older than she and had divined her talent, encouraged and helped her to write.

For her it was a liberation. Under her brother's guidance, she studied tenaciously to acquire the instrument of a clear and fluent language, free of the influence of dialect. And once she had it, she began to write short stories. She told the stories of the simple people she saw around her: the washerwoman, the peasant who came from the countryside to sell his produce, the servant girl who helped her mother with the domestic chores, the woman neighbor who confided her troubles to her. And into the telling she put all her impassioned rebellion against the condition of women at that time and in that society, all her sympathy for the weak and humble, who were destined to be crushed. These are the stories in *Pettini fini*, *Piccoli gorghi*, and *Ragazze siciliane*, leading up to her masterpiece, *A House in the Shadows*, with its bitter and sinister plot. But since her twenty years were also filled with a suppressed tenderness, she wrote children's books as well, giving expression to a gentler imagination.

Her manuscripts, submitted to the best publishers of the time without any recommendations whatsoever (Italy was then the small, modest, but honest Italy of the beginning of the century), were accepted and published, and were both a public and a critical success.

Meanwhile her father had received an appointment as school inspector, and was transferred with his family to various localities outside of Sicily: to Umbria, the Marches, Tuscany—which was always Maria's great love—and finally Naples, where they had a pleasant apartment on the Vomero hill overlooking the bay. In Naples the family enjoyed more tranquil times: as the years had gone by the disagreements and quarrels had abated, even if they had not disappeared completely. The financial situation had improved, and above all there was the excitement of visits by Maria's brother, who was living abroad with his family but came once a year to see his parents and sister, bringing his wife and two little girls—my sister and me, the nieces whom Maria adored.

Maria at the time, as I see her again in my memory and as I find her in the faded photographs in the family album, was a slender young woman with a small pale face and large luminous eyes, framed by a mass of fine chestnut hair. But this fragility concealed an uncommon strength of mind, the strength that she, a young lady from a good family who ought not even to have been aware of certain shameful things, needed in order to expose what lay hidden behind the facades of respectable houses, in which women were held in a state of subjection bordering on slavery.

Maria wrote constantly in those years, with increasing recognition. She received fan letters, as I remember, and carried on a correspondence with the leading figures of the Italian literary world. In particular, there was an exchange of letters with Giovanni Verga, of which unfortunately there remain only those from the inexperienced young writer to the illustrious Master who praised and encouraged her—letters in which one feels a throb of emotion that may have been the closest thing she felt to love.

Maria, who put all of herself into her books without asking anything else of life, might have been happy, if all of a sudden the dark shadow of illness had not fallen on her blossoming career.

Multiple sclerosis. A disease, still incurable today, that first takes away the will to write, and then slowly, as the paralysis proceeds, even the possibility of doing so. The fluctuations of hope and despair, the pilgrimage from one famous clinic to another, the uncertainties of mistaken diagnoses until that final and terrible one: all this is part of our family history. But only now do I fully realize the scope of her tragedy. She, who had rebelled with so much passion against social injustice, now rebelled with all her might against the injustice of the fate that had struck her. She refused to submit, she refused to lie down and die.

She kept on writing, slowly, painfully, working at the typewriter with unsteady fingers. But soon she could no longer do even that. Then she stopped struggling, and gave up answering letters and the requests of publishers. And little by little she was forgotten.

Her brother, who had so lovingly witnessed her literary debut, now witnessed with sorrow and anxiety her struggle against illness. But there was nothing that could be done. It was the 1930s: Maria, her parents having died, lived alone with a devoted nurse in the town of Pistoia near Florence, the last stop in her restless search for an impossible cure. She had a small garden on the same level as the house, which made it possible for her to go outside with her wheelchair. And my most vivid recollections of her are of that house and those years when I, then in my twenties, felt an affinity with her, with her aspirations and ideals, which persists to this day.

Maria was much changed, but though her physical

appearance had been devastated by illness, the strength
of her spirit was still the same. Except now it had taken
a different turn. Previously she had been at most a
lukewarm believer, but now sterile despair had given
way to the serenity of Christian resignation, a profound
faith that no longer sought in this world the redress of
injustice. She never complained, never spoke of her
sufferings, in order not to cast sorrow on our heedless
and rather selfish youth. I still remember how her ema-
ciated but still beautiful face lighted up with a smile
for me when I, holding her cold, inert hands in mine,
spoke to her of my hopes and dreams, which had been
hers too.

She died in 1944, at the time of the bombings of
Pistoia, separated from us because of the war, which
had split Italy in two. She died, so fragile and in need of
care, from the hardships of being evacuated to a peasant house. But in the hastily abandoned Pistoia apartment, her letters, files, and all her books were
destroyed, and it was like a second death.

Many years have gone by. Often, in the course of the
years, I would pick up the few things that remained to
us of her—some photograph or other, one or another of
her books of fairy tales dedicated to us children, with
those old dates: 1912, 1914, 1915 . . . And I would think
sadly that such talent deserved better.

Finally one day, among the recent publications of a
prestigious publishing house, I happened to come
across a little volume of short stories with her name:
Maria Messina. Inside, a brief note of commentary by
Leonardo Sciascia spoke of these stories rediscovered
by chance and judged worthy of being offered once
again to the Italian public. And he mentioned the mys-

tery of this woman writer who had vanished so quickly into the void.

I wrote to the publisher, putting myself at his disposal and offering to provide more specific information about the author and her work. Other reprintings followed, with growing recognition. Today, thanks to individuals who are sensitive not only to the clamor of voices in the present, but also to the call of subdued voices coming out of the past, this young woman's impassioned protest against the oppression of women in her time has crossed frontiers, and now oceans, and is coming to be heard very far from her provincial birthplace. Writing recently in *Le Monde*, the critic Anne Bragance, a specialist in Italian literature, remarked that a visit to this *House in the Shadows*, this sad house into which the writer introduces her readers by her art, while leaving them free to judge for themselves, is more enlightening, as well as more effective, for the cause of women than any feminist manifesto.

I think that for Maria Messina this judgment would have been the most heartening reward.

ANNIE MESSINA